CONFLICT
on Kangaroo Island

Stephen Crabbe

Yellow Teapot Books
Australia

Stephen Crabbe © 2016

The right of Stephen Crabbe to be identified as the author has been asserted in accordance with sections 77 and 78 of the Copyright, Designs and Patents Act 1988. All rights reserved.

Yellow Teapot Books
Australia

ISBN-13: 978-1535245579
ISBN-10: 1535245573

Historical fiction

To my friends Vivienne, Mare, Chuck and Lesley I am indebted for valuable support in the writing of this book. By sharing their responses and suggestions they gave me reassurance, and contributed to the improvement of the story.

CONFLICT

on Kangaroo Island

'Wind walk, wind walk ...' The child's small feet stamped in time with the syllables he chanted. 'Wind walk, wind walk ...'

The woman holding his hand smiled down at him. As they walked through the gentle wind his latest wordplay gave an extra newness to the day. It magnified the flashes of midmorning sunlight sliding through the silver-green leaves of the mallee gums. The snarls and sneers of the man they had just left, the stench of the blood and the skin stretched to dry, the unending demands from the two older boys — all of that seemed transient.

Hope sang here in the voice of the child at her side. Moments like this were too rare, evanescent jewels that occurred only when she was alone with him. For now, she could breathe freely and enjoy the lift in her cheeks that she realised was a smile.

'Look!' She pointed to the small clearing ahead with her free hand. 'Look, here it is!'

He pulled his hand from hers and broke into a trot. 'Three-tree! Three-tree!'

The breeze leapt suddenly to wrench a rattling gasp from the leathery foliage of the gum trees.

Chapter 1

Her fingers wrapped the inside doorknob the same instant his rapped the wood outside. Pansy drew startled breath at the thundering of the door as she opened it. A man, facing her. In the doorway. Not an arm's length away.

'Goot morning, madam. I look for der store manager but der shop door is shut.' He was stocky. A thick moustache drooped at the corners of his mouth.

'He'll open in a few minutes.' She stepped out and he stepped back. 'You're too early.' She took two paces past him, then thought better of it and turned back. 'Can I help you, sir?'

'Ah! Old horseshoes, madam? I haf come to buy!' He gestured towards the cart at the roadside. It was laden with bulging sacks.

She blinked at him. Horseshoes? 'Sorry, I can't help you. If you wait at the shop door my father might help you. I must hurry to work. Good day to you.' She strode along the road to the bakery tearooms, which she expected to be very busy by mid-morning.

Pansy's prediction was correct. At eleven o'clock the shop counter was lined two deep with people buying their usual bread and cakes, and at least six tables were taken by groups asking for Devonshire teas.

Steam from the big kettle billowed around her face. She tried to keep her eyes on the teapot as boiling water ran into it, and at the same time gave terse directions to the two young waitresses in the kitchen. 'Jenny, see to those two tables on the veranda — quickly. Susan, take the money from those people at the counter — and this time please be careful working out their change!'

Pansy Pearce lifted her laden tray and proceeded through the dining room. This Friday morning was favoured by some women of the district for regular re-acquaintance over tea and scones. Add a few January holiday visitors and it could make for a busy few hours.

She stopped at a table besieged by a party of older local ladies using a week's supply of received information in bursts of rapid-fire gossip. The only rule was that all ammunition must be spent before they rose from their places.

They all knew Pansy. 'Thank you, dear. Very prompt as usual.'

Another savoured the aroma of the plate of newly baked scones. 'Mm! Your baker knows how to make the best.'

'Yes madam. He's been hard at it since five this morning.'

'Well now!' One woman was about to direct the shooting of the group. 'The year nineteen-thirteen has begun with a little drama, hasn't it?'

2

'Yes!' Their line of fire was set and all eyes turned to Pansy. 'Have you heard about Connie Pincombe, dear?'

She let the empty tray hang at her side and stood erect. 'No, I don't think so.'

'The police have been inspecting her house and asking about her income. The poor dear! It's obvious she can't look after that little boy by herself.'

All murmured agreement.

'The constable said something about charging him as a neglected child.'

Pansy took a deep breath. 'So what happens to him?'

'Oh, he'll be taken into custody and put into an orphanage in Adelaide.'

'Best thing for him, don't you think?'

Again unanimous approval rolled around the table.

'Well, enjoy your morning tea, ladies.' Pansy went to the counter, noticing that people at another table were rising.

As she waited at the cash register her heart beat fast. Connie Pincombe's little boy! To be taken from his mother? An orphanage? Connie, just two years her junior, who had once worked with her in the tearooms; who had fallen into an affair with that possum hunter and then had to resign from her job because she was expecting a baby; who was abandoned two or three months after the birth, the man never seen again on the island. The little boy was a lovable smiling toddler now.

'Young lady? We're ready to pay!' A portly gentleman slapped down a pound note.

'Oh! Sorry sir! Too many problems to solve on a hot day.' It took her only a few seconds to total the amount payable, ring it up and count out the change to the customer. She was widely respected, even held in awe, for the speed and accuracy of her mental computation.

That was one of the qualities Mrs Harding, her employer, pointed out as they sat for a late afternoon cup of tea on the veranda. 'My girl, I believe you have all the abilities and the temperament you need to take over management of this business.' The older woman poured the tea into both their cups and ran her eyes over the newspaper spread on the table. 'It looks bad in Europe, doesn't it? Germany and Austria could join together to fight Servia, and Russia will help Servia, and France will join Russia, and then there's Turkey … As if things aren't already bad enough between Germany and Britain! Where does that leave all of us in the British Empire? God save us!'

Pansy frowned. 'A war, do you think?'

Mrs Harding shrugged, shook her head, sipped some tea and sat back to set her gaze on the young woman. 'Anyway, as I was saying, you have what it takes. Persevere! I struggled awfully when I was your age. It took me many years to see the path, but I can see now that when I chose Kangaroo Island as the place to establish the business, I chose well. There's a future here. More and more people from the mainland will come to enjoy the milder climate and the wildlife, to improve their health, to fish … Persevere, my girl, and you will enjoy splendid profits.' She raised her cup to her lips, took several slow sips, placed the cup back on the saucer. 'And *now* I will give you a chance to prove my judgement right.'

At twenty-three years of age, Pansy had received much approval from Mrs Harding since entering her employ, and there had been a vague hint or two of the possibility of advancement. This, though, was the first time the notion had become so explicit. A flutter of excitement erupted in her chest.

'I need to travel to Adelaide on business.'

Nothing new there. She had done so periodically for a few days at least twice a year. Pansy waited for more information.

'I have reached an age, however, at which more leisure is necessary. So I would like to combine it with my business in the city. Would you like to manage the tearooms and bakery while I'm gone for … say, a week or so?'

'Yes, I certainly would.' After years of waiting for this moment it was here. 'Thank you for your confidence. I promise to make sure everything runs very smoothly.'

'Good! I've booked a place on the *Karatta* for the day after tomorrow. The return trip might be a week later, but I'll decide that when I'm in the city. I'll send a letter to let you know.'

Already booked? So Mrs Harding had been certain her proposal for interim management would be accepted.

Pansy strolled, at the end of the busy day, rather than walked. She wanted to savour the sense of achievement derived from the conversation, and also to ponder a few extra tasks she must do while in charge. She decided not to head directly for home. The salty tang in the air and the easy glide of the pelicans circling above the sea combined to draw her downhill to the bay.

She ambled out along the jetty. A fisherman was gutting his catch of whiting and tossed innards into the water, where gulls swooped and squabbled to devour them. She watched the contest among the birds, how some inevitably dominated and others went without.

Like Connie Pincombe and her little boy. Anger sparked within her. No child should be torn away from his loving mother to be locked up in a soulless institution for years. The appalling injustice was intolerable. But what could be done about it?

Chapter 2

Ted Dodd watched the golden glow of sunlight fade steadily in his schooner of beer. This would be his last for the day. The shadows of the buildings on the road were long and he was tired. The prospect of again gathering the men and harnessing horses first thing next day was heavy in his mind.

His father, of course, was just starting to fire up for the night. He watched the man joking with his mates. When he spoke, they listened. They would argue about who would be the next to shout him a beer; he was that sort of bloke. And then before long they would all head off to some place for hours of card games. *A man's man*, they called him. Always chosen to be captain of football and cricket teams in his younger days; bringing his young son to watch every match and giving him special lessons on technique afterwards. And accepting the season's trophy on behalf of the team year after year. Ted's thoughts dwelt on all this for a minute. With that sort of example and encouragement all through his youth behind him, it was no surprise he had turned out to be a first-class sportsman himself. Well, that was the bright side of the story.

Ted downed the last of his beer, announced his departure and stepped off the veranda. With the rowdy pub voices dwindling behind him, he felt hunger pangs grow fiercer. His mother would have a big delicious meal for him, he knew.

It was one good thing about being back on the island. The reason he had taken some leave from his Adelaide job was partly to see his family again, but more importantly to sort out what to do with his life. He wanted to be sure where the future lay — with a return to the family business that his father's occasional short letters reminded him of, or with his secure position in Zoerner's city bakeries, which let him make the most of his football talents while his body allowed.

'G'day Teddy.' The voice came from behind.

He stopped. The low sun dazzled him when he turned. The silhouette was tall and lean. The strides were strong, the approach rapid. In four or five paces the person was close enough for him to avoid the glare while peering into the face. Was it Pansy? 'G'day,' he said.

'I haven't seen you for — five years, Ted? Seven?'

He shrugged. 'Yeah, about that. How are you?'

'Muddling through, I s'pose.' She looked up to the sky, grinned and set her eyes on his face. 'No, I'm actually doing very well, Ted.'

That direct, unwavering gaze of hers. He remembered it vividly from long ago when they were schoolchildren.

They resumed their walk, together and at a slower pace. She talked about her job, how she aimed to be the manager, and one day have her own business. He felt a little awkward conversing with a woman very close to his own height. Usually they could stand under his armpit.

'You're doing well in football, Ted. We notice your name quite often in the newspapers. D'you enjoy it?' Her face wore a pleasant enough expression. The shiny cheeks lifted with more than a hint of a smile.

And yet he felt he was under interrogation. He remembered that too. She was a very inquisitive girl, keen to know about everything and anything, even when it was none of her business. But he answered. 'Yeah, I enjoy it a lot.'

They halted outside the general store her father owned. Next to it was their house and on the adjacent property his own parents' place. His mother would be cooking his dinner now.

The clatter of hooves and jingle of harness turned their attention to a cart as it passed them, piled with bulging sacks. The driver was stocky with a big drooping moustache.

Pansy pointed. 'There's that man again! Did you know he's buying old horseshoes?'

'Yep. He's spent the last two days on the island.'

'He talks like a foreigner. What will he do with them?'

'He's an agent for the Germans. They take the horseshoes to Germany and use them to toughen the metal in their guns.'

'Germany?' Pansy shook her head. 'But I've been reading in the newspapers about Germany and Britain and other countries over there. They say we'll be in a war with Germany by next year. And we're sending horseshoes for them to make better guns?'

Ted shrugged.

They fell silent for a moment. The sun had sunk into the earth. In the still air a cacophony of drawn-out squawks drifted from further up the hill; black cockatoos winging their way to a roosting place.

Ted wanted to eat. 'Well, my tucker's probably on the table. Better be going.'

'How long will you be here?'

Ah! That was it, that way of tilting her head to one side as her eyes drilled into his. He remembered that from schooldays. It gave the sense that whatever he might say would be questionable.

'I've got a few weeks leave from work in Adelaide,' he said. 'But I'm doing some work for my father while I'm here.'

'Then I'm sure we'll find time to talk again.' She started to move away from him. 'I have some urgent business to attend to.' She gave the briefest of waves before striding in the direction of the police station.

He chuckled to himself. She'd feel at home there. He walked on towards his dinner.

Ted watched his uncle stride swiftly along the pile of bags, keeping tally on his fingers. 'About nine hundred and fifty hundredweight there.' He grunted. 'Not bad. I reckon with some extra work on Saturday we can get a few more cartloads down here before the next ship, eh?'

His father's eyebrows were raised as he glanced at Ted. The look meant *Your job*.

Uncle George saw it too and his face twisted in contempt. 'I'm sure you'll manage it, Ted — while your old man gets shickered in the pub all night and sleeps it off all day.' He cleared his throat and spat a yellow clot to the ground. 'I've just had news the price is up to four pounds twelve shillings a ton. That's the best ever. So I need those bags all stacked here before Monday!' He turned away.

The other two left the wharf and headed up the hillside street that formed the spine of the town.

Jack slapped his son on the back. 'Friday! Join me at the pub and I'll shout you a beer.'

When they sat at the bar Jack patted the young man's shoulder and slid another coin across the polished wood. 'A schooner each.'

The publican grinned as he brought out two clean glasses with a clink. 'G'day, young Ted! Good to have you back home! How long will you stay?'

'Not sure. I've got a few weeks off—Oskar Zoerner, my boss, is pretty generous. But they want me back to play football for Norwood again this year. And Mr Zoerner has arranged some accommodation for me at a very low rental.'

'We've been following the matches.' The publican set the two frothy schooners of beer before them. 'You're doing well, Ted. D'you reckon Norwood can win the premiership?'

Before he could hear the reply, some other customers snatched his attention with orders.

Jack nudged his son. 'You can probably finish that carting in one day if you grab all the boys. Get every dray moving. I need to spend time talking business with a few blokes.'

At that last statement Ted bit his cheek to stifle a snort before he spoke. 'The boys won't be too happy! We've been working bloody hard this week …'

'Well, be thankful you're not one of the poor buggers doin' the gumming! They have to work a hell

11

of a lot harder.' Jack gulped his beer. 'We have to get the shipments moving. The big man says the price for gum will go sky-high in the next few years. He wants all we can supply right now and he has plans for much bigger things before long.'

'Listen, who is this *big man*?' Ted had heard his uncle talk a few times about the person in Adelaide who paid him for the yacca gum. Sometimes he was called *the big man*, sometimes *Mr Mastermind*.

'Dunno. George doesn't either. Another bloke comes with the messages from Adelaide and reports back to whoever it is at the top.'

'All very murky! Are you sure you can trust them?'

'Your Uncle George is the one to handle all that, Ted. My job's to see all the stripping and carting is done right.' Jack patted his son on the back. 'And it's good to have you back working with me. Why don't you stay with us?'

The invitation triggered an unease Ted could not unravel. He studied his glass. 'Well, I'll … think about it.' He wiped his brow. 'It's really hot in here. Come outside for a while.'

Outside on the veranda a chorus of other drinkers greeted them with cheery banter. Jack Dodd revelled in his popularity. After a few days working with them, Ted realised it was his father's value in the business. Uncle George was different; as well as seniority of age he had business sense, a head for figures and paperwork, a flair for organisation. These were what put him at the helm of the enterprise. The important decisions came from him. He did not seem to like the work of building relationships with other people, however. For that—especially to maintain cooperation and hard work among the labourers—he needed his brother Jack.

This was a new understanding for Ted. Before leaving the island years ago he could think of both father and uncle simply as men whose lead he should follow to be successful in life. He worked beside them without question, mustering sheep and catching fish and harvesting yacca gum. Maturing in the city, working for wise Oskar Zoerner, training with great sportsmen and winning high esteem from thousands of football spectators—all that changed the way he looked at life, people, himself. Now, watching people on the island, he could start to make telling comparisons. He could see differences between his father and his uncle, qualities that made them tick as partners. He followed his father to the veranda and they sat on rickety chairs. They leant back against the wall of the pub. His father took out two cigarettes he had rolled and offered one. Ted shook his head. He'd given them up a few years back, following Oskar's advice.

'Mr Dodd?'

Jack looked into the unshaven face of a man obviously well past his prime, who drew up in front of them. 'Yeah. What can I do for you?'

'I hear you could give us a job.' The stranger stood aside and motioned to another even more unkempt man behind him. 'This is me mate, Bill. I'm Jim.'

As they shook hands with his father Ted guessed they were both past forty. Holes in their clothes. Angry red sores around the knuckles. These two didn't inspire confidence.

Jack shrugged. 'I'm not desperate for more drivers at present. Where you from?'

13

'We been workin' out at the salt lake. The pay's rotten. The living quarters are worse. We break our backs from sunrise to sunset and the only food they'll sell us is rice, bush biscuits and treacle. And we have to keep buying new boots and clothes 'cos the salt ruins 'em.'

Jack shrugged again. 'Why don't you go home and get better work?'

'Haven't got the money! A trip on the ship to Adelaide costs eleven shillings, mate.'

The other one chimed in. 'Listen, we're good workers. Nothin' could be harder than working in that saltwater up to your knees all day every day for months.'

Another man, one of Jack's gummer mates, lurched up to confront Jim. Beer slopped over the rim of his glass as he swayed.

'Hard work?' He spat on the veranda floor. 'You salties wouldn't know what hard work is! Try gummin' for a week and you'll find out. Yer a mob o' nancies, you are!'

A chorus of surrounding voices concurred. 'Piss off!'

Someone pushed Bill.

He snarled back. 'Fair go, y' bastards! We just want a job.' Fists clenched, he shaped up to a challenger.

Jack wanted no brawl. He eased his body in between the intending assailants. 'Easy now, fellers. Look, you two, I can't give you any work right now. If you're still around in a week or two come and ask me again. Something might come up.' He spread his arms to shepherd the pair off the veranda.

Chapter 3

When Pansy went to the police station, the thick wood of the door she pushed moved no more than the walls that framed it. The little stone building was occupied only three or so times a week by a policeman from Kingscote, unless urgent matters brought him out more often. Her intention had been to get information about Connie Pincombe's status in the eyes of the law, and about what could be done to keep her child in her care. But since the police were not available, she determined to act on her own assessment of the situation.

The next day she went to see Connie. When she knocked on the door, it clattered with a sound as flimsy as the rest of the place Connie and Benny Pincombe had to call home. It was in the backyard of a house owned by the Dodd brothers and rented out to several men who worked for them as gummers. Inside, the late afternoon heat was oppressive. It was no more than a tin shed, really, divided by wooden partitions into a bedroom and a kitchen. A brick lavatory stood in the yard, obviously used by all the men and Connie.

'Mr Dodd lets me use the laundry in the house.' Connie said this with a hint of a smile, as if the man were a philanthropist. 'We're not living like royalty, Benny and me, but we're not down 'n out either. I get a bit of money for laundry work from the boys in the house and one or two other people. I need a bit more than that though, before winter comes along.'

Pansy took up the little boy, held him in the crook of her arm and ran fingers through his tousled hair. She hopped around in a circle while singing 'Pop Goes the Weasel'. He giggled and hiccupped as he flopped around. She stood still and patted his back gently while he calmed down.

'Pansy ...' There was a quaver in the voice. 'They want to take him away from me. They can't do that, can they?'

Her helplessness sparked fire in Pansy. 'Not if I've got anything to do with it!' She thought for a moment. With Mrs Harding away she would be the manager of the business, a position of some power. 'Connie, I think I can help you earn an extra bit of money temporarily. And I reckon in a week or so you might be able to earn a lot more — permanently.'

Pansy hugged each of them before departing. She made a beeline for the police station, found it occupied and walked in.

'I believe, Sergeant, that you intend to declare Benjamin Pincombe a neglected child and take him from his mother? That would be a terrible thing for both of them. I suggest you reconsider.'

Sergeant Lawrence did what always worked when he wanted to control a situation; he narrowed his eyes and aimed an unshakeable stare. The two cold grey irises would send the spears of his authority into the

16

person before him. Since his arrival on the island his reputation and success in the job had been forged largely with this weapon.

'*I* will be the one to decide whether a charge is laid, Miss Pearce.' He hung each word in the air before her face, quiet, precise, firm.

The eyes meeting his did not blink, did not shift. The voice that answered was equally quiet, precise and firm, but female. 'If the mother is healthy and competent, and has an income sufficient to provide for her child and herself, the fact that she's single becomes irrelevant. There has never been any question of Connie Pincombe's health or competency as a mother …'

The policeman battled against an urge to blink. His authority was under assault—by a woman.

'… and she is now employed at the tearooms and bakery for enough hours per week to provide for her child. This *is not* a neglected child, and you know it.' Pansy turned to go, but then faced him again. 'If you need documents to substantiate her employment and income, as the acting manager I'll be happy to supply them. Good morning to you, Sergeant.'

The sergeant frowned as he watched the tall young woman disappear into the outside world. Circumstances had changed significantly since his constable's straightforward report of a neglected child.

Small waves flopping beside her and wind tugging her hair, Pansy revelled in the sensation of wet sand under bare feet as she ran along the beach. This was how to be truly alive! Through all of those years, until a few weeks ago, she had submitted to the rules young

17

ladies were expected to follow, except on the rare occasion she could escape notice. Running — really running — was effectively forbidden unless in emergencies or sport. Even in sport one was expected to not run hard; winning, after all, was not a ladylike pursuit.

No more bowing to all that. She might try, perhaps, to avoid other people while running, but if anyone saw they would just have to accept it. Pretence was now intolerable. Why? That was something of a mystery; she simply felt herself becoming a different person. All her life the deep urge to run and jump had mounted until it felt like a volcano ready to erupt within. From now on running would be fast and frequent.

The hard moist sand a little way beyond the sea's lick was the best. Here toes could bite in, soles stretch and spring. She burst into a sprint, lifting knees high and thrusting arms forward.

The powerful surge of air in her chest swept away detritus of tension. For a few seconds she felt the earth let her go, no sense of ground beneath, the strictures of the world severed and possibilities unlimited. Then, pulled back into her body by sudden weariness, she relented and slowed to a gentle trot.

Boulders ahead signalled the end of the beach and she came to a stop. Hands on hips and breathing hard, she looked around. The summer breeze idly toyed with her hair. Here along the north side of the island, the sea was tamer than on the south. A few times as a child she had been down there, and watched the Southern Ocean heave against cliffs to send glittering white spray high into the air. The water that now lapped close to her feet lay between the island and the

South Australian coast. Her scanning eyes caught a glimpse of dolphins, dorsal fins emerging momentarily here and there as the pod moved without hurry across the bay.

She turned away from the sea, her breath slowing, and looked past the dazzle of sand to where the terrain rose quite steeply, covered by low bushes and sedge. There, about a hundred yards away, was a familiar figure, tiny and white-clad against the mottled greys, greens and browns of the coastal vegetation.

'Amy.' The name leapt out with her breath, a wild whisper for the wind's ears.

She climbed the slope with vigour, noting the different feeling of the stone and soil underfoot. The young woman she approached was shorter, delicate of frame, with eyes as honey-brown as her skin. She sat on a smooth rock-face, glancing occasionally at the beach below before her fingers resumed swift strokes on a sketchpad. She was oblivious to approaching company.

'Hullo Amy!'

'Oh!' The pencil dropped from startled fingers. She jumped to her feet and gaped for a second. 'Pansy, what *are* you wearing?'

'Do you like it? I made it myself. You won't tell anyone, will you?' Of course Amy wouldn't, but even if she did, so what? It was time to stop letting people's opinions threaten. 'It's just to let me run freely, when I'm alone.'

Over several nights she had worked with the white linen, cutting and sewing to make the short-sleeved blouse and the divided skirt, hemmed some inches above her knees. The costume was very loose and unadorned by frills or trimmings.

19

'I changed my clothes in the little cave at the other end of the beach.'

Amy chortled. 'You always did like to run. I remember how Miss Gibson used to tick you off for challenging Teddy to races at school. You're a strange one, Pamela!' She laughed again and sat to resume her drawing.

Apart from her parents, Amy was the only person who ever called her by her full proper name, and even she did so very rarely. 'Pam' was used frequently by her sisters, but to the rest of the world these days she was 'Pansy'. That was due to Ted. In their schooldays he had decided the best way to save face was to dub her 'Pamsy', always pronounced with a sneer in the company of other boys. He later found 'Pansy' an even more effective label that would hint at some secret kink in her nature. Watching her almost six-foot sturdy frame stride along the street, he would snigger to his mates. 'There goes the little flower of our island, boys!'

She sat beside Amy and watched the picture emerge on her paper — sea, rocks, a small cloud near the horizon. Memories flooded her mind.

When the Dodd family had moved into town, Pamela Pearce had watched from behind the picket fence at the front of her parents' house, next to their general store. New neighbours seemed like a major change in her life: a new friend or two might come of this.

It was early on a Sunday morning and not another soul was visible in the main street. Two horses harnessed to the cart stood chomping from feedbags hung beneath their jaws while two men lifted furniture and boxes down to the footpath. A small woman with a delicate face looked anxious as she bustled between cart and house to take in items.

'Amy!' One of the men spoke sharply to a little girl clutching a ragdoll as she watched proceedings. 'Get out of the way now.'

A boy, much older, charged over and grabbed the little spectator by one arm. He hauled her into the house. Quite roughly, thought Pamela, amazed that Amy uttered no protest.

Pamela remembered opening the gate and walking closer.

When the boy returned, the man snapped again. 'Mary, go in and look after Amy! Leave this to us. Ted, take that crate from your mother.'

Pamela decided the man must be his father. He was very big. And he was darker than most people she knew. So were his family.

Ted looked eager to take the crate in his arms, but he was shorter than his mother. As she disappeared inside the house, he staggered beneath the weight.

Pamela darted over and grabbed the crate, just in time to prevent his collapse. 'You alright?'

'Course I am!'

The boy's snarl shocked her. She held onto her side of the crate and started to walk towards the house. A glance at the width of the doorway told her they would not both fit through together. 'I'll go through the door first.'

'I can do it myself! Clear off!'

Pamela was shocked. Why would he reject her help? She did as he said. She watched from a few paces away as he grunted and gasped, knees buckling, in an effort to manoeuvre the box through the entrance while unable to see ahead. A hand collided with the frame of the doorway.

'Aah!' Pain made his fingers release their grip. The crate fell to the ground and scraped his shins on the way. There was a crash, and then a number of tinkling sounds inside the box.

Ted's father stormed over to the crate and peered at the contents. 'Well, that's a few less plates for tea!' While the boy groaned on the ground, he stood with hands on hips and let words trickle down on him. 'Bloody good work! You want a hammer to finish the rest?'

As his father took the crate into the house, Pamela hurried to the boy and squatted down to peer at his blood-streaked legs. 'That must sting ... I'll get some water and clean it up for ... Hey!'

His shove knocked her over. 'Get lost! Leave me alone and mind your own business!'

Stunned, Pamela retreated and stood to watch on the veranda of her house. The vague hope of new friendship shrivelled. A minute later, her mother pulled her inside to dress for church and her world felt quite unaltered.

There were at least some ripples of novelty the next day at school. Seven year-old Pamela arrived well before bell time as usual, in search of games which allowed her to run or jump or throw things with other children. Those activities made her feel alive. In the small area of hard levelled ground where girls often played hopscotch she found chalk markings complete and ready for a game, but no one was there. Strange. In fact, there was not one person to be seen in the yard.

Yet there were voices, many and lively, coming from the other side of the school building. She followed them and found over a dozen kids crowded together. At the centre of attention were two, her new neighbours. The little girl sat on the wooden seat, head bowed. Below her white hat black locks curled over her cheeks. Several older girls hemmed her in. Close by stood her brother, arms folded and feet firm on the ground, looking squarely at a few other boys.

'So, Ted, you wanna have a few kicks?' The speaker bounced a football and caught it again, barely moving his eyes from the new boy's face.

Ted's expression was of clear indifference. 'Oh s'pose — if you like.'

The first boy nodded once before trotting off in the direction of the open yard, bouncing the ball every few paces. His friends followed.

Before he stepped after them, Ted's eyes met Pamela's. She saw recognition on his face, followed within a split second by a sneer. Then he was gone.

Pamela stared after him. Less than two minutes yesterday, about one second today. That was all the time he needed to hate her. Why?

His little sister, meanwhile, remained surrounded by other girls, eyes downturned.

'Come on, don't be scared,' one of the biggest girls said in a far-too-kind voice. 'Tell us your name. We want to be your friends!' She tried to hold the little girl's hand, but it immediately jerked away.

'Her name's Amy.'

All heads turned to Pamela as she shouldered her way through them to stand next to the new girl.

'How do you know?'

'She lives next door to me. She moved in yesterday. Didn't you, Amy?' Pamela squeezed into a narrow gap between Amy and a girl sitting beside her.

23

The new girl looked at Pamela in surprise at the question. She gave a tentative nod and turned her gaze once more to the ground. There was a moment's silence while the others took in this unexpected relationship.

The big girl chirped with exaggerated eagerness. 'Hey Amy, come and play hopscotch with us!' When answered with a shake of the head, she looked at the others. 'All right, let's leave her to Pamela.' And away they went to the games area.

Amy gradually accepted Pamela as her friend in the ensuing days but joined in very few activities with other children. She was often by herself at school, wandering around the trees and bushes along the fence. Her fingers might explore the surface of eucalypt trunks and lift the leaves of wattles. She would squat to peer at tiny bells of correa blossom or stroke thick moss on a branch long since fallen.

Sometimes she would appear to be talking to herself. Yet she seemed not unhappy, her face often lit by a smile never seen in interactions with others at school. Once or twice Pamela overheard girls mutter that Amy was probably an aborigine, but nothing more was ever said about it. On the island, that sort of ancestry was a topic usually avoided in conversation.

Meanwhile Ted made himself not only popular but a leader among the boys. Tall and sturdy for his ten years, he proved himself the strongest kick with the football and the fastest runner. His words were few but heeded; his preferences signposts to his peers. He seldom looked at Pamela except to make a face of open contempt, often followed by some snide remark which his mates would greet with laughter. Before long all the boys treated her with the same scorn.

24

Ted, Pansy recalled, was eighteen when he left the island. Along with her family, she went to see their neighbour off. The expression on his face, as he boarded the ship to the cheers of a rowdy mob of men led by his father, was a mixture of pride, uncertainty and excitement. He was a local hero, off to Adelaide to take up a position in the Norwood Football Club's league team, as well as a job in Zoerner's bakery business.

It was almost at the same time that Pansy left her father's business. She walked boldly but alone, and observed by only her mother, who stood on the veranda watching her eldest child disappear up the road to Mrs Harding's tearooms and bakery. Pansy's quest was for independent success in a field where her intelligence and managerial capacity would be better rewarded.

All those years past seemed to tumble around her now in the breeze that came in fits and starts here on the coastal slope. One moment it would make Amy's black tresses dance playfully, and the next it would drop them. Her concentration was intense as she studied waves or landforms for a minute and then firmly transferred their lines to the paper. It was a marvel that anyone could capture a landscape this way: a single line crossing the page in two seconds was obviously the crest of a wave; a little shading conjured a jutting splinter of layered rock into the vista. As Pansy sat next to her, wonder at the girl's skill competed with admiration of the delicate brown forearms, the glint on her cheek.

So magic was the day that she felt they had sat like this for hours when several voices tumbled to their ears. Two men and a woman were picking their way down the slope towards them.

'Good day to you, ladies!' The man looked like the oldest of the trio with his well-trimmed grey beard, slight paunch and tasteful hiking attire. 'A wonderful place, this.' He seemed pleasant, even avuncular.

'Especially for an artist.' The woman approached from behind to look over their shoulders at the sketch. 'An artist of considerable ability too, young lady!'

Amy arose with a little giggle and clutched the pad to her chest. The dark complexion could not hide the blush on her cheeks.

Pansy knew it would be hard to get two words out of her until she felt comfortable with these strangers. She turned to the older man. 'Good morning. Out sightseeing, are you?'

'Well, yes, but in a professional manner. We're here on an extended visit to study flora and fauna on the island.'

'Ah, so they're back together again, then! I'm happy to hear that.'

The visitors stared at her. The bearded man cocked his head in question.

Pansy shrugged. 'Well, we've seen Flora around now and then—looking sad, mind you—but last we heard, Fauna had cleared off to the mainland.'

Amy shuffled her feet and looked at the ground, unable to suppress a giggle. Seeing the quiver in her shoulders, the man's face broke into a grin of understanding, and the woman behind him chuckled. The younger man, serious from the outset, hung back from the group, lips tightened.

'Are you all making a scientific study?'

'Largely so, yes. We've come from Adelaide. Allow me to do the introductions. My colleague, Mrs Margaret Crump, is a highly regarded botanic artist. This young gentleman ...' here he turned to beckon his morose companion, '... is Arthur Brewster-Leigh, a brilliant natural scientist from the University of Adelaide.'

Pamela saw the young man nod curtly while taking a quarter turn away from her gaze. Brilliant by qualifications, perhaps, but no shining light in conversation. She turned back to the speaker, raising her eyebrows.

'Oh! And I am Kenneth Maine. I'm here as a representative of the Royal Society of South Australia. Have you heard of our organisation, Miss ...?'

'Pamela Pearce. And this is Amy. No, I'm afraid I don't know the Royal Society.'

He explained how the Society comprised learned people whose interest was in all science, with a special focus on the State. They were campaigning to have the Government reserve a large portion of Kangaroo Island for the protection of indigenous species. The man warmed to his topic as he spoke, and moved on to details about the areas and species under consideration.

As his enthusiasm waxed, Pamela's attention waned. She noticed from the corner of an eye that Mrs Crump had put Amy sufficiently at ease to get the sketch pad into her hands and leaf slowly through. She lingered over some of the work, making small noises and nods of approval. They conversed in murmurs while Maine's exposition ranged over ospreys and spinebills, orchids and samphire, and the species of small emu made extinct by the first European visitors to the island.

Every head turned when the third member of the party interrupted from a few paces away. 'We'd better move on. It's close to noon.' He spoke in jabs with an intense reedy voice.

'All right, Arthur. Just allow us a minute, please.' Mrs Crump sounded like a mother soothing an impatient child. She turned back to Amy. 'My dear, you have a real talent. My sort of art concentrates on producing objective details of a plant, but I do know good landscape art when I see it. Who has taught you your skills?'

Amy shrugged with a hesitant smile. 'Well … I haven't really had lessons.'

'Oh, come now! There must be at least a little tuition behind work of this quality?'

Amy blushed as she shrugged again and shook her head.

'Goodness gracious!' The older woman leafed through the sketch book for a second. 'You know, Amy, I would very much like to see more of your work while we are on the island.'

Amy blushed again. 'I would be honoured to show you my paintings at home, Mrs Crump.' She explained where she lived and agreed on a late afternoon visit for the next day.

Watching the trio depart, Amy wore a grin broader than any Pamela could recall on that delicate heart-shaped face. She was exhilarated by recognition from a famous artist, and Pamela could not help grinning with her.

The party began to move away but suddenly Kenneth Maine stopped and called back. 'Oh, and by the way, ladies, we need to gather some support from the local people. You will think about our proposal for the island, won't you? I hope to talk with you and others again soon.' He waved and followed his companions out of sight.

Chapter 4

James Pearce mopped his forehead with a handkerchief. 'Simply not enough room for it all.' He buried his face in his hands. 'It's almost impossible to get to some of this stuff. Jammed in too tight. But I can't afford to reduce stock, because every now and then someone comes in with a big order. And I really don't want to build another storeroom!'

'You don't need to. All of that stuff can fit in here easily.'

Hands on his hips, James faced his daughter. 'What? I've tried every which way, Pamela! Do you think I'm stupid?'

Pansy said nothing for a minute. As he watched, she stepped to a corner and looked from one pile of boxes to another, measuring with her eyes the lengths of their sides and mentally transferring them to different spaces on the floor. She stood beside several boxes marked *Stationery* and studied them, drumming her fingers on one.

'And Pamela, if you're about to tell me to move those again, don't bother … Oh, now hold on … No,

Pamela! Those boxes weigh at least a hundredweight each ...'

But his daughter bent, grasped one of the boxes of paper and carried it to a corner of the storeroom. She repeated this with one box after another, arranging them so that those on top of a stack were lighter, easily moveable by anyone wanting to get into the heavy ones at the bottom. Scattered, loose items were placed in half full cartons or crates. Smaller containers were shifted from floor to shelves.

'Pamela, please! You'll hurt yourself. At least let me help ...'

Though his ostensible concern was for her wellbeing, she knew from the subtle change in his voice that he was annoyed. It had always been like this. He saw her solution was going to work and resented it.

'It's all right,' she grunted. 'I'm almost finished.' Her strength was at least equal to his — another thing he resented — and giving verbal explanations would take more time.

Pansy worked swiftly and precisely. And then it was done. All the merchandise was accessible and there was a clear path where two people could move side by side.

'So you don't need another storeroom, Dad.'

He stepped along the aisle she had made, spreading his arms to test the clearance. He looked stacks of boxes up and down silently. Eventually he nodded slowly, mouth squeezed tight. 'I think that'll work.' He walked ahead of her out of the storeroom and into the shop, muttering. 'Thank you.'

This was all familiar to Pansy. Years ago she would have simply accepted it, but now his behaviour seemed quite childish. He always wanted to be the one to direct, to solve problems, to make the crucial decisions. To accept that his daughter—even at twelve or thirteen—could do such things just as effectively was more than he could bear. Pansy, of late, found it increasingly ridiculous that she was part of this family; or of the Kangaroo Island community, for that matter.

She could remember, though, a real sense of belonging at times in her younger years, when she stayed with her mother's parents in Adelaide for holidays. Unpretentious and hardworking people from northern England, they were, Adelaide residents since the early colonial days. How she had begged her mother to let her go to them at the end of every school term! In most matters James Pearce was allowed to rule with little argument, but not in this. 'The girls will know their grandparents, James. They will come with me to Adelaide.' That very rare firmness of her mother's voice as she stood before her husband was unforgettable. She ensured the daughters frequently spent time in the city with their grandparents before the old people passed away.

Nostalgia gnawed at her as she observed her father taking his silver watch from the pocket in his vest. He looked at it and frowned. 'Now Pansy, I have things to do. What was it you came to tell me?'

His terse words jolted her back to the present. She summarized her chance encounter with the three visitors from Adelaide and their proposal for an island sanctuary and sanatorium.

'I thought it all sounded quite exciting,' she concluded. 'It would bring lots more visitors from the mainland and that would boost business for you, and the tearooms, and boat owners. Mr Maine says they need support from residents. I just wanted to let you know.'

He heaved an exaggerated sigh. 'You thought it *exciting*, did you? And the farmers will be excited too, won't they? When they're told they should not harm the possums and wallabies that destroy their crops? That they should not harvest the yacca gum or distil eucalyptus oil? Perhaps they shouldn't clear their land at all. There's a marvellous message for farmers!'

The sarcasm grew more blatant with each new sentence he uttered, his hands outspread in a gesture of disbelief. She had given him a perfect opportunity to exact revenge for the humiliation he felt in the storeroom a few minutes earlier.

She opened her mouth to explain the proposal would not necessarily be so all-encompassing, that it might very well open new doors for new enterprises.

He held up a hand, palm towards her. 'This island was settled for farming and fishing, Pamela. Some farmers have already heard about the preservation plan. Joe Benson told me the other day what he thinks of it—and I won't repeat his words. Don't expect people to be *excited* about what they hear at this public meeting, young lady!'

As Pansy watched him turn away and make a great show of being busy with the cash register and account books, she was satisfied she had acted wisely by walking away from a job in his general store. She could have made so many improvements to the business. He would realise what he had lost one day, when she made a successful career for herself elsewhere.

Mrs Crump arrived alone at the Dodd house. Pansy, driven by curiosity as usual, had made a point of being there with Amy. And it was not only curiosity: she wanted to witness professional acknowledgement of Amy's ability. Amy's life to this point was not adorned with praise and honours. Quite the opposite, in fact.

'So, my dear,' the woman said as she looked through the paintings, 'what are your favourite subjects? I see here some very interesting coastal landscapes ... lovely palette on this one ... and those rocks are *excellent!*'

'I like trees and plants best.'

'Aha! My speciality. Show me some of those, please.'

The two were immersed in their discussion for a long time. As they murmured and pointed, exclaimed and nodded agreement, Pansy watched Amy's face grow flushed, not only with pleasure but also with plain excitement. In Margaret Crump she was finding, for the first time, someone who understood what she was trying to do with her art. Matters of perspective, composition, colour, brush technique — all was beyond Pansy's grasp, and after a while she wandered from the room.

The rest of the house was very quiet. Amy's father was out at work. There was no sign of her mother.

In the sitting room she let her eyes roam idly until they came to several framed photographs hung on one wall. She had been here and glimpsed them at other times, of course, but now, unaccompanied, she could study them at length. Here was a wedding picture of the two parents, very stiff and formal. Then the family all together, the children all of school age. And here ... this one was more recent. The young man stood erect, limbs muscular and shoulders broad beneath the team guernsey. The football tucked under one arm seemed tiny against the mighty hand that spread over it. The face, though not smiling, suggested a strong self-assurance. But Pamela could remember when it was shadowed by self-doubt.

Teddy. Or Ted, as he was now known. How that face had flickered with shock and annoyance when she beat him across the playing field at school. It was bad enough she was younger; far worse that she was female. A *girl* had proved physically superior! It was not on a school day and so Amy was the only witness. No one else ever came to know about the contest, but Teddy's own knowledge was enough to trouble him. None of these pictures betrayed that, of course; they were all testament to his sporting glory. Now she travelled through memories as she studied the photographs.

'Ted's back on the island. Did you know?' Amy's quiet voice from behind returned her to the present.

'Yes. I happened to meet him the other day.'

Mrs Crump was just behind Amy, her appraisal of the artworks apparently over.

'Well, Mrs Crump, is she Australia's Leonardo of the future?'

The restraint in the lady's little smile could not diminish the excited glitter in her eyes. She lowered her gaze for a second in thought, and then spoke slowly. 'Amy's work shows a great deal of natural talent, and technique which I would have thought impossible to achieve on this island without professional tuition.' She looked steadily at Amy for a moment and then back to Pamela. 'It demonstrates an inborn gift one encounters in one person out of millions.'

Pamela clapped her hands. 'I've always thought so myself, but it needed someone like you to confirm it. Thank you, Mrs Crump.' She watched the flush and smile of pleasure spread over her friend's face.

The older woman held up a finger. She was not finished. 'But there is something else apart from technical achievement.' Here she turned pointedly to Amy. 'What you have shown me is evidence of an extremely *rare* understanding of your subjects, my dear. Oh, I'm not talking now about the landscapes, but rather the plants. As a botanic artist of long experience and considerable understanding of the demands of the profession, I see in you one who is fully aware of the minutest details of each flower, bush or tree. And you perceive the unique *beauty* of each species. I also see you have developed outstanding *skills* for depicting them. In all that I feel we are alike. But ...' She inhaled deeply and searched the air for words. 'You do something *else* in your work, something I do not. You paint each subject like a *living character*, almost as if ... as if you could *talk* with them.' She looked at each of them briefly. 'I do hope that doesn't sound silly.'

Pansy said nothing. The woman was obviously an unquestionable authority on artistic matters, but surely painting and drawing was simply a matter of observation and technique one learnt somehow. Talking with plants? This was drifting into silliness.

Mrs Crump moved to the door. 'Well, I must be away. My colleagues will be expecting me for another short survey of species before sunset. We need more facts we can present to the government. And ... oh yes—I should have mentioned this before! We have been asked by some of your local residents to speak at a public meeting. They seem keen to discuss our proposal for the island's future. I do hope you will be there, both of you!'

As they walked slowly out of the house and onto the street, Pamela lagged behind the others. She stared at the ground, a thought forming. It crystallised and she called out to the other two. 'Hey, wait! Mrs Crump, I've had a brilliant idea!'

Black cockatoos moved their wings so lazily that, at times, they seemed to just hang in the air for a second or two on the way to their roost in the last rays of the January sun. Their prolonged squawks and squeals fluttered down like falling leaves onto Pansy. The unhurried mood found an echo in her stroll away from the bakery tearooms after a very busy day. Busy but satisfying. She was convinced she was managing the place well.

There was no hurry either in the movement of the broad-shouldered figure crossing the road ahead. Ted Dodd. Finished work, finished a few beers at the pub. Heading home for tea. His father, of course, would still be in the pub with no intention of going home until well after midnight. There would inevitably be a poker game somewhere once the pub closed. It was good to see Ted wasn't following the same road in life as his father.

'G'day Ted.'

'G'day, Pa ... um ... '

Was he unsure of the name he should use for her? She chuckled. 'It's all right. Everyone calls me Pansy these days.'

His head bowed for a moment. 'Oh. And you don't mind?'

He was feeling awkward, she could tell. Reluctant as an adult to use the name he had pinned to her in childhood as a deliberate insult. 'I'm used to it. My parents are practically the only people who call me Pamela.'

'Righto.' His voice subdued. Nodding slowly in thought. Taking time to adjust to the change in relationship.

He looked her in the eye then. 'So … you've been working late?'

'Yes. I'm managing the business while Mrs Harding's away. I need to spend time after closing to go through the books, think about what orders I'll have to place—that sort of thing. What about you, Ted? Are you busy?'

'Too right! And it'll only get busier. Uncle George is trying to expand our gumming. They say the Germans are offering higher prices every month.'

There was the word again, *Germans*. Was the whole world hinging on them?

'Dad's got the job of going around to try and get contracts to clear land of yacca. A lot of property owners aren't saying yes until Joe Benson signs. They reckon he knows best, and he reckons they should just keep handling the yacca themselves. He hates to see small businesses swallowed up to make a big one bigger. You know?'

She nodded. 'He's got a reputation for that, and for persuading other men to think the same way. A natural leader, they call him.'

'Well, he's not making Dad happy!' Ted gave a wry smile. 'He was cursing Benson the other day.'

'Listen, what do the Germans want the gum so badly for? I know it's good for varnish …'

'Oh, yeah, that's the usual story. But in Germany they're using the stuff to make explosives—you know, for bombs and big cannons.'

Pansy threw her hands into the air. 'God save us! Government people are saying the Empire could be at war with Germany before long. What's the Germans' problem?'

'I know lots of Germans in Adelaide and they're good people! My boss, Oskar Zoerner, for example. His grandparents settled on the mainland in the colonial days. He says about ten percent of South Australia is the German community …'

'Yes, yes, I know. But I'm talking about the *nation* Germany. First we're selling them our horseshoes to make better guns, and now we're selling them yacca gum for ammunition. Arming the enemy? Ted, do you see something silly about that? I call it insane, myself!'

Was he going to respond to that? She would never know, because an outburst of male voices outside the pub seized their attention. The usual group of drinkers on the pub's veranda were on their feet and circling a man. They jeered at him and blocked every move he made to pass by.

The sound that leapt from Ted's mouth was half gasp, half grunt. 'Hey, what …!' He staggered backwards from the thrust of Pansy's shoulder as she began to run towards the stoush.

She reached the group, sensing Ted's approach behind her as she moved. The circling men were obviously intoxicated, some swaying as they pushed the besieged victim savagely to each other. He staggered and straightened again, only to be shoved towards the next man. This went on until he fell hard to the ground.

'Stop!'

They ignored her. No time for more words. She stood behind one man who was shorter than her, put both hands on his shoulder, positioned her leg behind his shins and pulled him backwards. The man landed heavily on his back. That won their attention.

'Let Mr Brewster-Leigh go about his business, or I'll be reporting you all to Sergeant Lawrence for assault.' Pansy drew herself erect to catch her breath.

From the downed man came snuffed snarls and half-stifled expletives. His mates barely moved as they stared at her. She faced them squarely, feet spaced securely and arms slightly bent in readiness for further action.

The hiatus was enough for the spindly victim of the circle to scramble to his feet and collect spectacles and hat from the dirt.

The group began to rebound from their surprise. 'That piss-weak little poonce is trying to take away all our jobs!'

One heavyset man stepped towards her with a threatening growl, but Ted leapt to block him with a league footballer's granite shoulder.

Pansy stepped into the ring and put a reassuring hand on the shoulder of their target. 'Are you all right, Arthur? Off you go then.' And she looked around at each face in turn before continuing. 'I know all your

40

names. I won't forget them if anything more happens to this man.' She strode through them and back towards her parents' house.

Ted joined her. 'Aiming to increase your popularity, are you?'

'The man is not harming them! He might be unusual, but that's no excuse for bullying.'

'So you *know* him?'

She said nothing.

Chapter 5

As Pansy trod the steps to the tearooms entrance, Mrs Harding's parting words echoed in her mind. *You're ready for this, my girl. You're highly efficient and practical, and you can also organise other people very well. That's all quite rare in young ladies of your age.* Then she had lowered her voice. *One word of warning, however. Keep a special eye on the other girls — especially young Jenny. I've had occasion to reprimand her about avoiding work lately. She might try to take advantage of my absence.*

The good sense of this advice soon became evident. Seeing only three customers in the dining room, Pansy went first to the office to attend to some paperwork while staff went about their jobs. Half an hour later she walked through the scullery and kitchen, only to find no staff. She moved to enter the dining room and collided with Connie Pincombe. Connie had experience as a waitress before becoming a mother, but she was obviously flustered right now. The young woman held a tray piled with used crockery which would have fallen from her hands but for Pansy's fast reaction. She steadied the tray and noted that Connie's usually milky cheeks were as scarlet as a rosella's breast.

'What's the matter, Connie?'

'The tables are filling all of a sudden. It's really hard for me to keep up!'

Pansy looked out of the kitchen doorway to see nearly every seat taken. A touring group must have come from Kingscote. The holidaymakers were coming to the island in droves this summer, as news spread of its milder climate and fresh ocean air.

'Why are you by yourself, Connie?'

'Jenny said I could handle it for a while because there were hardly any customers. Then they all suddenly started coming in.'

'I'll make sure you have help in a minute or two. Now just work at a pace you can handle.'

Pansy let her continue and went searching for Jenny. She found the waitress at the back of the shop twining herself around a young man.

'Close attention to customers, Jenny, is indeed what we want.' Pansy seized the girl's gaze with her own. 'But it should be given with pencil and order pad at the front of the shop!'

The two unwound themselves and faced her. Jenny was twenty, the recipient of her favours probably ten years older. His shirt was frayed and his hair needed a rake. He smirked and cocked his head in defiance.

Pansy stepped close to him. She had to look down slightly to make eye contact. She spoke in a quiet level tone. 'You can sit at a table with the other customers, or quit the premises before I tell the police you're trespassing. It's a two-second choice.'

The man's posture and smirk collapsed. He turned and slunk out through the back door.

Jenny moved to pass Pansy in the direction of the front of shop, but was restrained by an arm. She pushed. The arm did not budge.

'A quick word, Jenny.' Pansy sought the younger woman's sullen eyes but met only evasion. 'That man is best avoided. He's one of those possum hunters the farmers are complaining about, the gang that bags more than possums. They have no respect for anyone's livestock and belongings, and he'd probably regard a girl the same way. Please be careful.'

The girl contemplated her feet.

'Right, then. The tables are nearly full. You shouldn't have left Connie by herself. Off you go now!'

So Mrs Harding's prediction about Jenny had been right. Should the behaviour be reported? Dismissal from employment could be a huge blow; there were few openings for young women to be gainfully employed around town. Jenny could be even more open to temptations like the one interrupted just now.

The bustling trade allowed no time for pondering the matter yet. Pansy helped to take orders until people at most tables were happily eating and sipping their tea, then moved behind the counter to take payments and make some brief conversation that might leave a good impression to linger in the minds of visitors. At the same time, she tried to keep the staff under surveillance; particularly Connie, who, despite her experience, should not be placed under too much pressure in the first hours of her re-employment.

There was a lull during the luncheon hours; tourists were probably eating at the hotel or their guesthouses. The mid-afternoon proved no less hectic than the morning, more tourists having arrived in town. As she worked, Pansy made a mental note to recommend Mrs Harding request the Tourist Bureau to send advance notice of arrival times of such visits. It would enable better preparation for efficient catering, which would be in everybody's best interests.

It was a relief to say goodbye to the staff as the sun slid down the summer sky. She sat at the desk to do the bookwork. Shadows began to creep through the window as she finished. She put down the pen, placed the lid on the inkwell and leaned back in her chair. The question lurking all day in the corners of her mind now rolled into the centre: What more could be done about the situation of Connie Pincombe and the child?

Perhaps it would have been more proper to wait for Mrs Harding to return and then recommend that Connie be employed at the tearooms. But that would not forestall the police charge of negligence, and so Pansy had put Connie on as a part-time member of staff. Yet, to meet the real needs of a mother and child, a full wage was necessary. Mrs Harding was an understanding and generous soul, and she would surely take into account that Connie had been one of her waitresses before being put into the family way. She would certainly see the rightness of the action.

The impact of a new wage on the business ledger, however, might not seem so justifiable. To offset that, why not suggest dismissing Jenny? After all, Mrs Harding herself had voiced unease about the girl's attitude and work habits. She could be replaced by Connie. Pansy felt sure she had the solution, when her rumination was interrupted.

'Good afternoon, Miss Pearce.'

45

She jerked into an upright position. The male voice hammered from the office doorway.

'Sergeant Lawrence, good afternoon. What can I do for you?'

'I couldn't see anyone at the front of the shop, so I walked through to your office.'

Pansy left her chair and stood to face him.

He continued. 'Miss Pearce, a person has reported to me that she saw you behaving in a very unseemly manner in public. She states that you ... ah ... manhandled several men. In fact, that you caused one of them to fall hard on the ground. I'm told he has a very nasty bruise. What do you say to that?'

'It's nothing compared to the way they were knocking Arthur around! Someone had to stop them immediately, and words wouldn't have done that.'

She saw the policeman's jaw clench. His grey eyes stared into hers. 'Miss Pearce, I am a very busy man— too busy at present with investigation of arson and assault. Much more serious than ... the incident we are discussing.' His chest swelled with an exaggerated deep breath and subsided slowly. 'But I have to warn you, Miss Pearce, that your behaviour lately is unacceptable. Your interference in police business regarding Mrs—or is it *Miss*, I wonder—Constance Pincombe, followed by what seems like public brawling ... well, it means I must put you on my list of persons to watch.' He tried to lift himself to a greater height. 'You are in a very serious position, Miss Pearce. Do you understand that?'

She grunted with a smirk, never dropping her own gaze. She would not succumb to his drilling eye and self-important attempt at intimidation. 'A serious position is exactly where I constantly aim to be,

46

Sergeant. A *flippant* position in life would be inexcusable.'

His lips parted, but no words emerged.

Ah! Could it be true? Did those grey eyes not only blink twice but widen? Had she deflated him a little?'

He cleared his throat loudly and half-turned on a boot heel. 'Your father is a very respectable man, Miss Pearce. I know he will be very disappointed by your recent behaviour. I hope you won't make it any worse.' He stomped out.

So! A *very serious position*, was it? Marked by local people — a certain section of them, anyway — and now she was warned and under watch by the police. Simply for going to the aid of three people who were unjustly trammelled by society. Continue or surrender?

As she locked up the tearooms and said goodbye to Dan in the bakery, Pansy knew she could not give up. She felt sure she had an answer to Connie's situation. Well, to the financial aspect anyway; the matter of regular care of the child was still to be settled.

On the walk home her mind still rang with the sergeant's voice. *Your father will be very disappointed.* Did that mean her father would be informed of her 'position'? And what was that he said about being too busy investigating arson? Who had been burning someone else's property? And *assaults*, did he say? Much was happening, much to learn.

47

Chapter 6

Ted saw his father emerge from Uncle George's office and stand, hands on hips, to turn his face up to the clear January sky. His teeth were bared. He bent and grabbed a rock. With a savage growl, he hurled it as hard as he could. It bounced off a tree trunk.

Ted waited on the dray, reins in hand. His father charged across the yard towards him, snarling to himself. Ted picked up only an odd word or two: 'contraptions' and 'smart-arse'.

'Let's go boy!' His father jumped onto the seat beside him. 'There's a bloody big stack of bags to collect out in the paddock.'

He said not a word on the way. He sat erect and rigid. Now and then he would rub a hand irritably across his face and bring it down with a slap onto his thigh. Ted said nothing; he just let him stew.

But later that day he met Uncle George and found a clue or two as to why his father was behaving that way. Ted was at the wharf, heaving the last sack of gum from the dray onto the pile.

'Ted, I want you to come with me for a few minutes.' It was a flat statement that did not invite questions.

After a five minute walk through town Ted found himself directed to enter a boarding house, one of several in the town.

George spoke to the plump woman who owned the place. 'I need to arrange accommodation for an important businessman. He'll be arriving in a few days. He needs a room for two nights with the option of more.'

Told a room was available, George asked to see it. 'I need to know it's suitable for him.'

The woman showed them into the nearest room. 'They're all occupied until tomorrow,' she said. 'The gentleman who has this one is a scientist. He's out every day, so I'll show you this one. The others are all much the same.'

It was a clean room with the necessary furniture in good condition, but no more. George sat on the bed to test its springs. He opened the wardrobe and chest of drawers, glanced behind them to gauge the cleaning, tested the window to be sure it would open and shut easily.

The woman seemed affronted by all this. 'Yes, cleaned daily, sir!' Her voice was loud with indignation. 'And I open the window every morning to let fresh air through for a while.'

George grunted. 'I think it should be satisfactory. We'll book it.'

Outside the boarding house Ted felt his uncle's restraining hand bring him to a halt. He turned an enquiring eye to the man beside him. Uncle George was as big and strong in physique as his father, but very different in other ways; much quieter, not eager to mix with the boys for more than a minute or two. He spent a lot of time in the office poring over books, letters, newspapers.

'Ted, I want to explain a few things to you. I think you could shoulder a bigger role in the business if you choose to stay with us. So I'm going to tell you a bit about where we're heading.' He touched Ted's chest with a cautioning forefinger. 'Now this is private information, mind. Do not let anyone else know. Right?' He gave a wry grin. 'Your father knows most of it, of course. But between the two of us, I don't think he's the man to manage this business. And I reckon he understands that. He's fine at supervising the boys and working with the horses, but times are changing and we need a different sort of man to deal with them. Someone like you.'

Ted said nothing. It was flattering, of course, that his uncle thought so highly of his potential as a businessman. But something else, something vague lurked behind the flattery and it made him uneasy.

'You know we have an arrangement with a company in Adelaide that buys our gum and sells it to Germany. The man at the top doesn't like to be identified. Oh, he obviously knows just what he's about and he makes the big decisions, but he insists we deal only with his general manager. That's the bloke who's coming to visit me. He doesn't want to stay in the grand hotel up on the hill. It would make him too conspicuous. That's why I'm booking his room in an ordinary boarding house.'

He went on talking as they moved without haste along the road back to the wharf. He explained that the market for gum was perfect for a huge expansion of the operation on Kangaroo Island, and that was just what the 'Big Man' in Adelaide intended to do. The Germans were expected to offer more and more for purchasing gum over the coming few years. Big Man would slash the overheads by sending ships to more diverse points on the coast, so that overland transport routes could be shortened. The efficiency of carting to the ports would be greatly improved by the introduction of motor lorries to replace horse-and-dray transportation. One lorry could do the work, it was often said, of six drays.

Ted had a flash of understanding as he heard that. He knew why his father was in such a foul mood. Motor lorries — those 'new-fangled contraptions' that he often heard his father deride — would replace horses and carts and greatly reduce the number of men needed for carting. So that was what his father was angry about when he came out of the office earlier in the day. He hated any kind of motor; the engines of the gum jiggers were simple enough, but even they made him nervous. The thought of learning to drive and maintain motor lorries would certainly daunt him.

'With gum prices higher than they've ever been,' Uncle George went on, with a tap on Ted's chest, 'and less to pay for carrying the stuff, we can offer more money to the landowners. The man wants us to become the only gumming contractors on this island. Every bloody yacca will go into *our* jiggers!'

The younger man listened without uttering a word until his uncle finished.

'Ted, just think about it, lad. You're bright, healthy and young enough to make this the start of a marvellous business career. Just think it over, eh?'

Ted stood on the wharf next to his dray and watched him mount his horse and disappear up the road through the town and into the bush at the top of the hill. His uncle had never before spoken to him like that; at length, adult to adult, open about business facts and possibilities. Even more unusually, he was suggesting his nephew could become a manager of the whole show. A quiver arose, deep in his body. The idea excited him, but he felt guilty at the same time. He shook his head hard, trying to clear this confusion.

After driving his dray back to the gumming site, with the falling sun in his eyes, he watched three men at work on the yacca bushes. Some were trimming the leaves and burnt edge of the stems. Others axed the bare stems to make the gum fly off into a hessian cradle standing at the side. Another pair of men operated the jigger machine to remove the rubbish, and then put the remainder through the winnower, which separated the coarser material from the finer gum.

Jack Dodd wielded his axe as they did, halting now and then to walk among the gang. 'You're doin' a bloody good job, boys!' He slapped one on the back. 'We'll have another forty hundredweight ready piled up in a day or two. Let's keep workin' our arses off and I'll shout you all a few beers on Friday!'

'Bloody bewdy, Jack!' They would swing their axes faster, or more briskly carry the bags of winnowed gum to the pile awaiting the carters. 'How about today too?' And they would all chuckle and fall silent again, working on.

Listening to the laughter and cheers from some of the men, Ted had to give his father credit for the way he dealt with them. He got his way by working with his muscles just like them while joking, flattering, and sympathizing. No hint of aloofness or giving orders. No indication he was putting schemes into action. In other words, he didn't act like a boss but built and manipulated camaraderie for his own ends.

On the other hand, Uncle George was rarely seen out in the backblocks among the dirt and sweat; his office was clean, quiet and structured. The two Dodd brothers were different in almost every way. So different, in fact, that Ted wondered how they had been able to cooperate as business partners for so many years. Perhaps each needed the other too much to let a rift separate them.

Ted and another driver finished stacking the bags of gum on their drays. 'We're going, Dad. Last load for today.' The two teams of horses heaved forward.

How much more efficient this could be, Ted mused as he flicked the reins. If roads were better maintained, if roads were made to closer points on the coast where the bags could be loaded onto ketches … But that all depended on government initiatives.

Transport in Adelaide was swinging towards motor vehicles. Oskar Zoerner, his city employer, was now also moving in that direction; his bakery products would be carried more by motor lorries than by the horse-and-cart method that had done the job since 1836, when South Australia had been founded. So would motor driving lessons be required when he returned to the city?

Perhaps the job in Adelaide had served its purpose and should now be discarded. After all the years of steady work and successful dedication to football in the more formal society of the big smoke, the notion of resuming his place on the island in the family business seemed worth contemplation. An offer of some share of control of the enterprise now seemed likely. Honesty forced him to admit that, these days, occasional thoughts were arising of long-term prosperity and a career outside sport. But there had to be more than that to life.

Marriage? Now that was a different thing. Finding the right woman among the few eligible here on the island appeared very difficult. Alluring recollections came to mind of dances and parties in Adelaide, replete with an endless variety of pretty girls.

He was now rattling through town to where the gum was to be left near the wharf. A tall woman in a dark blue frock and broad hat strode into vision ahead of him. She turned her face and trained a pair of steady eyes on him. Pansy. He raised a hand in greeting and then she was gone.

Motor cars. That should be a topic of discussion on the island, where many horses and the drays they hauled would sometimes churn the moist soil of tracks into a useless quagmire. Lorries would certainly be a way to make the transport of gum quicker and, in the long run, cheaper. The younger of the Dodd brothers, however, would impede any such progress in their business.

Ted and the other driver worked together to unload their bags of gum. Finally, he stretched his back, wiped his brow and sighed. 'Done for the day, mate. Let's put these horses away for the night and grab a beer, eh?'

Chapter 7

Under her bare feet the sand was hard and smooth. The still air was filled with the cries of a mob of Pacific gulls around the rocks at the far end of the beach. She sprinted hard, relishing the sensation of cool sand under her toes as they sprang into each new stride. The boulders of the promontory loomed and she let her legs slow to a halt. Her body could pant hard now, each explosive exhalation satisfying. The last few days at the tearooms had been hectic, with several visits by charabancs full of tourists swelling the clusters of local residents and more regular customers from the Hill View. Two of the girls at the bakery counter were off work with sickness and so she had to serve there too. This run on the beach was now working all of the tension out of her body.

The shrieks of the gulls and the sound of her own heavy breaths were not enough to stop her ears grasping another noise quite alien to the situation. She held her breath for a few seconds to attend more closely. Yes, it was the sound of some kind of motor, alternately murmuring and roaring, somewhere up there on the high ground way above the beach. She had occasionally heard similar sounds—a motor-launch coming to berth in the bay, a tractor shared by several farmers—but not quite this sound, and certainly never around here.

At the cave she donned only her shoes; the change of clothes could wait a few minutes. A glance at the terrain and height of the slope suggested a vigorous two-minute ascent.

The last thrust took her over low saltbush and then she stopped. The motor roared again but was still not visible. Following the sound, she trod through bushes and found her feet on a road. She stared. There, not fifty yards along the way, was the source of the noise.

A man in dark blue work clobber was too preoccupied to notice her as she walked towards him with a casual air. She stood behind him and stared in silent admiration for a few seconds while he bent over the engine with a spanner.

'That's a beautiful thing you've got!'

He jumped and spun around, knocking the spanner out of his grip. It fell onto his foot. 'Ow!' He squatted to attend to his foot but could only stare at the grinning young woman in outlandish clothing. 'Who are you?'

'Most call me Pansy.' She stepped forward to peer at the machinery. 'But *Pam* if you like. What's this thing here? What makes it move like that?'

The man stood up, a grimace still on his face with the pain from his foot. 'It's very complicated, young lady—too hard to explain in a minute or two.'

'I haven't seen you before. Did you bring it over from the mainland?'

'I'm employed by the government to maintain and drive it.'

'I see. So while you drive, who rides?'

With a smirk the man looked her up and down. 'Nosy young thing, aren't you? Is that the traditional local costume you're wearing?'

She laughed heartily. 'I wish I could say so! I wear it to make running easier.'

He blinked, wrinkled his brow in query, and then decided not to voice his thoughts. 'Uh … look, I have to get on with my work. Nice to meet you … Pansy.' He only half-smothered a snigger and bent over the engine again.

The motorcar was dark blue, island dust failing to extinguish its shine. And it bore a silvery name at the front, between two large lamps of gleaming brass. 'Maxwell'. She pronounced the name slowly. 'Hullo, Maxwell!' She inspected the vehicle from the front, the back, and each side. She stood on the running board and peered inside, ran a palm over the leather seats. She gripped the steering wheel thoughtfully. 'Mmm …'

She stepped back off the running board. 'Oh! Oh, excuse me!' The man had been behind her, watching. On spinning around she glimpsed the hungry-dog expression on his face, before it squeezed out a grin.

Eying him squarely, she drew herself erect. He was no taller than her, possibly even an inch shorter, in fact, and now, as she narrowed her eyes and cocked her head slightly to the side, she detected a slight unsureness stealing across his face. The moment of advantage.

Her eyes on his, she lowered her chin and spoke in a low, conspiratorial drawl. 'I find Maxwell *very* attractive.' Her hand reached to the side and stroked the blue body. 'I'd love to have a ride on him. My *first* ride ever.'

He fingered his chin. 'Well ... I do have to go for a test run. But you must promise not to tell anyone. You understand? I could get into a lot of trouble if word reached my boss.'

The next few minutes proved an unforgettable thrill. With the wind in her ears, the motor growling one moment and dying down the next, Pansy did her best to listen to the driver explain why he and his vehicle were on the island. The Maxwell 1913 Tourer was the latest in its line, imported from the USA and purchased by the South Australian Government for the use of parliamentarians and top-ranking public servants.

Gerald was the man's name. He explained how his job was to care for the car and be the chauffeur. At present he was driving for two very important men on a tour of inspection for a week or more. He spoke with the air of one who possessed every fact worth knowing. 'This island's close to ninety miles long and maybe forty across at the widest part. A big area for only 1,300 scattered people. They figured a motorcar would be the best way to manage the travelling.'

The South Australian Attorney General, Mr Homburg, was at that moment with Mr Butler, Commissioner of Public Works, in a meeting with a delegation of local settlers to discuss how the government might help to improve economic activity in the area. Gerald was giving the engine 'a bit of a going over' before collecting them in an hour or so.

'Your island roads are pretty rough on a motorcar,' he said as he swerved to avoid a pothole.

She trained her eyes directly on his face and donned her sweetest smile. Although the car was bumping furiously over a patch of corrugations, she summoned the most girlish voice she could manage. 'I say, Gerald, the way you handle this beast is so unbelievably clever! How long did it take you to learn to drive a motorcar?'

'I spent six months over in Melbourne, training in Australia's best motor academy. Studied motor mechanics at the highest level. Driving trials in conditions most people shouldn't even consider tackling. Extremely rigorous, it was, Pansy. Not many come out of it with qualifications.' He was sitting higher in his seat now, chin raised, glancing at her from the corner of his eye.

'Gerald?'

'Yes, Pansy?'

'Do you think you could show me how to drive? Oh, I know ...' She touched him lightly on the arm. 'I could never be as good as you, but maybe just a little taste of what it's like?'

He grimaced. 'You have no license, right? And this isn't my car. If anyone saw us I could lose my job!'

'Oh, no one would see us out here, Gerald! And ...' She paused. 'Well, I'll never again have the opportunity to learn from a master of the motor like you.'

An hour later Pansy brought the Maxwell to a halt at about the spot of their first encounter. As she pulled the handbrake tight, Gerald drew a deep breath and sank back into the passenger seat.

'Gerald, thank you *so* much. I'll never forget that experience.'

'Nor will I.' He gave her a thoughtful look. 'You learn more quickly than anyone I've tried to teach. And you seem to have strong nerves. I must admit to being a bit anxious at first but now ... well, I'm impressed.'

Waving goodbye to Gerald, Pansy thought how wonderful it would be to have the opportunity to do more driving one day. Of course, she would need a license. An idea began to form.

Mary Pearce smiled wryly at her daughter. 'Yes, Pamela, I suppose it *is* nice to have a little boy playing in our house. Your sisters are certainly very pleased with the arrangement.'

'Thank you for agreeing to it, Mother.' Pansy watched Clarissa, youngest of her family, happiness glowing on her face with a rare brightness, roll a ball to the one and a half year-old. He was probably getting far more attention here than his mother could give. 'Once Connie has earned enough money to pay a minder he'll be off your hands.'

'Not so easy, Pamela. I can't think of anyone else around town who's likely to be the minder. And you know your father isn't going to tolerate this arrangement for long. He likes to have at least two of us in the shop through the day.'

'We'll muddle through somehow. I won't stand back and let them take him from his mother.'

Clarissa gave a shriek of laughter. 'Hey, Pansy, he's got the idea now. Watch!'

Her mother frowned. 'The name is Pamela, young lady!'

Pansy smiled as the little boy laughed in triumph, stopping and returning the ball without fail. Then he picked it up and threw. Clarissa had to leap giant steps to stop it from crashing into the crockery on the sideboard.

'Clarissa!' Her mother jumped to her feet. 'That's enough. If he's going to throw you must take him outside.' She looked at her eldest daughter. 'I'll do what I can, Pamela, but don't expect it to last.'

'I must get back to the tearooms. I told the girls I'd be just a few minutes.'

With Mrs Harding away in Adelaide, Pansy felt she could step out of work for a short time if circumstances warranted. She had left clear instructions so the waitresses would be productively occupied, but at that time there were no customers. Now, however, some chairs could be occupied. She strode swiftly along the road to the tearooms while assessing her situation.

The woman placed the little boy's hand into his big brother's. She wrapped the larger blood-smeared fingers around it. 'We'll take him to his magic spot, shall we?' She stroked the little head once.

The man heard and stepped forward. He spat on the ground at her feet. 'Magic, woman? Don't you never say that word again! You let my boy be strong, d'you hear, woman? And you ...' He jabbed a thick forefinger into the chest of the older boy. 'You're no baby now. You stay with me and keep skinnin' these wallabies.'

The mother and little one walked away down the narrow track and disappeared among the mallee trees.

The older boy watched them go.

'Come on, boy!' The man took his wrist and pulled him away. 'We have to get the hides off the rest of these wallabies.'

Chapter 8

The institute hall was packed; though it was a small building, she had rarely seen the walls lined with standing bodies. Pansy surveyed the faces—nearly all men, nearly all island residents—to detect signs of their mood. There would be a wide division of opinion, she knew. There were people who thrived on visits by tourists, and a good number were hoping to make the island a huge sanatorium to attract convalescents and others seeking to generally improve their health. On the opposite side were those whose focus was farming and fishing, along with a group keen on developing tree plantations. It was a potentially volatile mixture. The proposal of a huge area for the preservation of trees, bushes, animals, birds—in other words, everything natural—could be like a lit match to gunpowder.

In the front row she could see the smiling faces of Kenneth Maine and Margaret Crump in genial conversation with people around them. Next to them Arthur Brewster-Leigh's head twitched constantly but never faced anyone; he checked the pocket watch in his palm at least twice a minute. The Dodd brothers sat near the back. Ted was with them.

Joe Benson was right in the middle of the audience, face like a convulsing walnut, in agitated discussion with several other men around him, swivelling to now one, now another. He seemed anything but happy. Was it perhaps because of the fire on his property? Gossip had circulated a few days ago that the destruction of his shed with a cart and other items had been arson. That was, of course, what the sergeant had alluded to in his visit to her at the tearooms. Reason enough for Benson to be in a bad mood, but as a dedicated farmer he would feel no happier about the subject of this meeting.

A handful of people at the entrance tried to squeeze into the hall. Faces here and there were turning to her with frowns or raised eyebrows. She retaliated in kind, shooting glances back at them. No doubt they considered it odd, some perhaps even impertinent, that a young woman with no standing in the community should appear—by herself and of her own initiative—at a meeting such as this. One or two of those faces showed ill-disguised derision. Attitudes born in long gone schooldays could apparently persist forever among some men.

The owner of the Ocean View Hotel, the town's high-class and most expensive accommodation for visitors, rose to face the gathering as someone rang a handbell. 'Ladies and gentlemen, please stand for Song of Australia.'

They all knew the first few lines; it had been taught to every schoolchild in the State for many years. *There is a land where summer skies / are gleaming with a thousand dyes ...* Voices began to drop out after that, leaving the dozen or so more conscientious souls to finish the customary two verses.

Pansy held back a giggle as she remembered the parody that circulated through schools: *There is a land where all the flies / crawl up your nose and in your eyes …*

The hotel owner began the proceedings. 'Ladies and gentlemen, I thank you for attending this meeting, as the subject of our discussion is extremely relevant to every resident of Kangaroo Island.' He went on to suggest that the mild climate and sea air made the place a perfect location for rest and convalescence. 'Given the appropriate facilities and professional doctors and nurses, we could see scores of people every month coming for that purpose. Moreover, the whole island might become the prime destination for tourists from the rest of Australia, lured by the rugged beauty of our coastline and the wonders of our animals, plants and trees.'

Vigorous applause broke out from a few small groups in the hall. The rest of the audience remained silent.

'I grant you that the island is also excellent for farming and fishing. I see no reason why such activities should not continue alongside these new proposals. If that is to eventuate, certain steps must be taken. Here today we have a group of very learned and accomplished people, who are eager to advise us on the matter.' He introduced the trio and invited each to speak in turn.

Kenneth Maine's open, genial manner found favour among the islanders. He outlined the diversity of flora and fauna to be found on Kangaroo Island. He explained how, many years before the British colonisation in 1836, men had come to live on the island to hunt seals for their skins, which they sold to visiting traders. Some of these men were escaped convicts from Van Diemen's Land, later named Tasmania. They brought with them aboriginal women from that island and kidnapped others from the mainland of South Australia. They hunted animals for meat and established small farms.

Kenneth Maine paused there, before making a point in a louder, more emphatic voice. 'All that shooting and trapping, my friends, made a huge impact on the native species. The island's unique dwarf emu very soon became extinct. The local variety of kangaroo was almost eradicated.'

Maine now dropped his voice a little. Pansy noticed how this prompted the audience to look at him with more intense concentration. 'Now I fully understand that Kangaroo Island produce is badly needed by the rest of this State. Farms, orchards, horticulture—they are all necessary and there is no reason why they should not go on.' He waited while his audience gave a short outburst of applause, and then continued. 'We all know that the harvesting of gum from the grasstrees provides important material for manufacturers of varnish; and the picric acid derived from the gum is in great demand overseas for making better explosives.' The authoritative voice launched into a great crescendo. 'Kangaroo Island is producing nearly all of the world's yacca gum! Of that, ladies and gentlemen, you can be proud!'

Pansy saw George Dodd clap loudly at this, sweeping the hall with his gaze. Many others responded to this cue by immediately joining him. At the front of the room, Maine nodded and smiled; he seemed, so far at least, to be making few enemies, if any. The man was obviously a practised orator.

The noise died and the speech resumed. 'The problem with the gum harvest, however, is that it completely destroys each plant. It is a species of xanthorrhoea apparently peculiar to Kangaroo Island. If the harvesting persists at the present rate, the species may be extinguished. I hope we can agree to preserve a large area of the island to protect the species. There is some hope, too, in work going on in Adelaide to develop an alternative method of gathering the gum, a method which will not destroy the plant.' Succinct and convincing, the end of his speech earned almost unanimous applause. Even so, Pansy thought the faces of many people suggested they clapped more from politeness than agreement.

Margaret Crump waxed lyrical about the beauty of bays, wild seascapes, bushland scenes and particular plants and animals. She reeled off names of serious artists who had exhibited the results of their visits to the island, and she reported their comments. She talked about the possibilities for extended tours by groups of art students and amateurs from across the nation and abroad. She stressed that 'all would be seeking accommodation, meals, and other services to the benefit of island businesses'. This address, like Maine's, was less than ten minutes in length and received a polite applause from most. A group of ladies, whom Pansy knew to be especially interested in cultural matters, clapped more vigorously.

When Arthur Brewster-Leigh leapt to his feet, however, the atmosphere changed. Pacing continually, he ranged over the uniqueness of numerous plants and animals. His hands flew about as he placed a concept before the audience, planted a species name here and another there, and pressed each point into place in the air before him. Again and again he hammered the point that the island might be the world's last bastion of species under threat on the Australian mainland. Repetition and convoluted sentences whirled through the air of the hall. Long scientific words never before encountered by the listeners accumulated in piles.

Arthur's gesticulations grew wilder by the second. His voice crept higher in pitch.

An interjection hurtled from the middle of the audience. 'Rubbish! We have to clear the land to grow our crops. We're not bloody scientists—we're farmers and fishermen. That's what we're here for. Kangaroo Island is settled for farming!'

The young scientist on the stage fell silent. His arms froze in the air. He did not move for several seconds. Nor did the people around Pansy: they were waiting.

Arthur leapt into an impassioned tirade. 'Science must advance! We must continue to gather knowledge of our native species and impart it to the people.' The reedy voice jabbed emphases in every direction. The thin body jerked and twisted as if he were surrounded by enemies in mortal combat. 'And this island presents us with the greatest opportunity to do so …'

George Dodd reached across to a man seated a row ahead and tapped him on the shoulder. The man gave George a nod, and himself tapped another.

Arthur was almost shrieking now. 'We must preserve all the species on this island so we can study them, allow schoolchildren to come from the mainland to learn about them. Further clearing of land must be made illegal ...'

'You're a halfwit! We produce the food and goods to keep people alive. They'll learn nothin' if they're starvin' to death!' It was the first man George had alerted.

The second one joined in. 'Them wallabies are vermin!'

One by one, other voices added to what fast became an uproar. George Dodd said nothing, but sat and watched with a smirk of apparent satisfaction.

The thin young man on the stage pounded a fist on his other palm as his voice was drowned. His face reddened with fury. He bent forward, and bared his teeth as he yelled.

Pansy glanced again at George. Yes, he had planned for this to happen on his silent signal.

The chaos now drowned Arthur's speech. Abruptly he hopped down from the stage and strode towards the nearest heckler. He yelled in the man's face, only to receive a sneer and be waved away. He went down the aisle to another. The jeers and gestures continued.

Joe Benson stepped out of the crowd into the aisle and stood to confront Arthur. Barely a yard apart, they stared at each other. Arthur closed his mouth and brought his feet to a halt. As they remained in this unspoken confrontation, others in the audience realised what was going on and the voices died.

Was this part of George's strategy? He was frowning. His glances at faces around him silently invited them to explain what Benson was doing, but the only answers were shrugs and headshaking. So he had not planned this particular stand-off. Benson was the independent initiator of his own show of opposition to Arthur Brewster-Leigh.

69

Arthur stood fixed to the spot, his voice stilled. He breathed hard and stared at the rugged older man who, hands on hips, barred his way up the aisle. Kenneth Maine and Margaret Crump had left their places and now moved up behind their young colleague, anxiety all over their faces.

'Who do you think you are?' Benson spoke with his usual gruff voice, but in an even tone. 'This is an island of producers. We've been here for a long time, some of us for generations. We work hard for our living, mate.' He held out his hands, huge and gnarled as a mallee root. He continued more loudly. 'The story's all here in these hands. Now you, with your silky white hands, come here 'n tell us we should just stop!'

Arthur replied without hesitation. 'This island is unique. Here science and education can advance to a greater extent than anywhere else in the country! Plants and animals that are on the verge of extinction anywhere else could be safe here. Like the dunnart, for instance. If you would just stop removing vegetation — especially the xanthorrhoea!'

'You mean the yacca? You want us to stop gumming?' Benson was coming close to a boom, anger darkening the leather of his face. 'You want us to stop the work that makes it possible to pay for expanding our farms! For the sake of little rats — bloody vermin!'

Arthur's mouth began to work in fury but his voice seemed choked with the rage of frustration. His glasses were close to falling from his nose because of the frenetic twitching of his head. Exasperation was too much. A squeal escaped from his throat and he lunged forward, hands clawing at the older man.

Kenneth Maine was quick enough to seize his shoulders and hold him back.

'You brainless fool!' Arthur screeched, trying to shrug off the restraining hands. 'You can't think beyond your profits, can you? You think nothing of butchering a whole species just so your money pile grows. It's you and your kind who should be killed off!'

Arthur tried to lunge again and Maine struggled to keep a grip on him. Other men around Benson stepped forward, obviously ready to use their hands on Arthur. Dozens of voices put the hall into an uproar.

Benson held up his arms out at each side and the men stayed back behind him. 'It's all right, boys, he's no danger. Let's get out of here. This is a waste of our valuable time.'

The owner of The Ocean View flung a feeble voice into the throng. 'Ah ... Shouldn't we all sing God save the King first?'

Benson turned to leave the hall, but stopped abruptly to stare at Jack Dodd who was leaning nonchalantly against the wall beside the door. Pansy could not see all of Benson's face, but his body posture seemed very intense. He did not move for at least five seconds, while Jack first projected bewilderment and then tried a placatory smile. Jack stepped away from the door and Benson strode through.

What was that all about? Hadn't Ted said something about the two men being at loggerheads?

Benson left the hall, followed by his supporters. A number of others remained inside, drifting over to the side wall to cluster and murmur around the Dodd brothers.

71

The hotel owner mounted the stage and suggested that, in view of the heated mood of so many, it might be best to adjourn the meeting until a date to be decided.

Pansy stepped up to Margaret Crump. 'That went well!'

The older woman blinked, frowned and looked up to scrutinise the deadpan face. Then her brow relaxed as she recognised the irony. 'Oh!' She chuckled briefly. 'We have some minds to change, haven't we?'

'A different choice of speakers might help.'

'Mmm … our Arthur, eh?' She turned her eyes to the young man, now pacing the floor in a remote corner of the hall, slapping a chair occasionally and grumbling to himself. 'Yes, in retrospect I admit we should have realised his temperament was not the most likely to win this audience.'

The pair fell into a defence of their colleague. 'A sterling intellect,' Kenneth Maine was anxious to point out, 'but ardent, to say the least, when he finds a cause to fight for.'

'His intentions are admirable …'

'Yes, yes! He wants to achieve wonderful things …'

'But to bring change about in society, there needs to be a different way of communicating one's ideas and ideals.' Margaret shook her head. 'He comes from a very wealthy and influential family in Adelaide. They've rejected him. We try to give the poor chap the friendship he deserves, to protect him from himself. But we can't be with him constantly — we must return to Adelaide the day after tomorrow …'

'And,' Kenneth Maine's grim tone interjected, 'Arthur has decided to stay here longer — without us!'

Pansy shook her head. 'That sounds ominous. Perhaps I should try to keep an eye on him.'

The others thanked her in fervent unison. Pansy turned to leave but Margaret's drew her back.

'Oh Pansy, that brilliant idea you had — we've agreed to take it on! Let's make a plan before we return to Adelaide. Well done, and thank you, my dear!'

Pansy smiled about this as she walked home. Amy should be informed now about the *brilliant idea* that her paintings would be at the centre of a public exhibition to help persuade people of the importance of protecting the island's wildlife. A magnificent way for Amy to begin to establish her reputation.

Meanwhile, though, there could be trouble for Arthur: he would find it very easy to bring violence upon himself on this island.

Chapter 9

James Pearce drew himself erect and faced his eldest daughter squarely. 'No, Pamela, no. If this were a short term emergency I would not object, but it is not. It's about the child's whole future. The Christian thing to do is to face the facts and deal with them in his best interest.'

'Father, Connie has an income ...'

He held up his palm like a shut door in her face. 'This young lady succumbed to temptations and allowed a vile man to use her. Since the irresponsible fellow abandoned her, left her with the poor innocent fruit of their lustful dalliance, she must now agree to the only course of action which can provide adequate care for the child until he can care for himself. The police are right, Pamela. The boy should become a ward of the State.'

'Once Connie is earning enough money she can pay for someone to mind him ...' Pansy heard herself repeating the plan she had outlined to her mother, knowing her father would reject it outright.

'Pamela, even if she finds a minder — and it's next to impossible, as you well know — the person may give next to no care, while taking the money and eventually demanding even more. Or one day be too sick to do the job, or find herself having to move from this town, or ... No, the child will have a very unstable life if it's left to her.'

'If Connie paid Mother, or Louisa, or Clarissa ...'

His voice grew louder. 'They're needed in the shop, Pamela! This business is growing and requires all available hands.' He drew a deep breath, fixed his gaze on her and delivered the bitter, weighted syllables she knew would come. 'Which do not include *your* hands, of course.'

She spun about and strode out of the shop. It was just like when she was twelve. The door slammed and she blinked in the glare of the summer sun. He had always clashed with her. He could never accept a child in the shop who could operate mentally with money and measurements faster than any adults, or solve storage problems better. When she showed she could control stock, order the right quantities at just the right times, he would just deny it. Oh, he struck gold when Louisa and Clarissa were born, didn't he? Meek subordinates, those two, to perpetuate his command of business and family, and later marry to give him grandchildren.

Little wonder that eventually she could stand it no longer and steered a course outside the family business. Mrs Harding took her on as a waitress and quickly assigned her to higher duties to make use of her talents. This, of course, peeved her father even more.

The barbs of his resentment stung as she made her way to the house next door. Mary Dodd, Amy's mother, might agree to mind Connie's little boy.

Pansy reached the climax of her sprint as a silver gull cried above her head and a tiny wave collapsed on the sand to her left. Filling with a fountain of exultation, she let her strides slow and shorten. A few yards from the boulders at the end of the sandy cove she stopped, bent with hands on knees, and submitted to the tirade of fast breathing that now took over her body. With each exhalation the tension dammed up over the last week ebbed from her.

Half a dozen leaps, boulder to boulder, took her to the little cave. She scanned the landscape for witnesses before stepping inside and changing from homemade running clothes into conventional frock. Shoes and hat in hand, she headed up the boulders to the sandy slope covered with coastal saltbush, clumps of needle sharp rush and succulents. Very little air moved in the late sunlight; bees droned around the radiant pink flowers of sprawling pigface. A smile stretched her face: all problems could be solved.

At the top of the rise she let her eyes wander over the sea, the cove, the further coastline. The sun had about two hours to sink over the west of the island — enough time to saunter homeward by a longer route. Time to ruminate over all that had crowded into her life of late, all terribly muddled. She turned and walked towards the mallee country.

A mile or so brought her to a track that wound past Joe Benson's property on her left. He had cleared much of it, and she could just glimpse the roof of his house in the distance. A rugged individual, Joe. So independent he seemed to attract enemies. That was, no doubt, behind the strange silent confrontation in the institute hall.

The track headed into an area of quite thick scrub. The mallee trees spread their pale trunks like skeletal fingers supporting clumps of foliage. Among them to her right was a group of yacca bushes, some of them six feet high or more. Their lower parts burnt by bushfires, they stood like black torsos crowned by huge masses of spiny hair.

She stopped. A thin human figure was moving between the yaccas. It stooped and straightened, stepped and stopped in stiff slow movements. Like a weird insect.

Pansy left the track and walked closer. The figure disappeared. Reaching the yaccas, she peered behind one of the younger plants whose lower bristles spread and drooped to touch the ground.

'Aaah!' The man flipped from his facedown position to lie on his back with legs and arms in the air as if to ward off a predator. He stared at Pansy, face contorted with fear.

'Good day, Arthur.' She smiled to give as much reassurance as possible. 'Hard at it, eh?' She guessed he'd been investigating life beneath the overhanging spines of the yacca. 'It's all right. I'm Pansy Pearce, remember?'

It took a few seconds for Arthur to abandon his defensive position. He stood, lifted his hat from the ground and faced her. Still recovering from the shock, he blinked often. His chest rose and fell rapidly.

'You startled me.' His mutter was barely audible.

'Sorry about that, Arthur. So what are you doing?'

77

'Part of our survey. I'm very interested in the fauna that live in relationship with the *xanthorrhoea* species.' His breathing was now returning to a more normal rate. 'That means the yacca.'

'So you were looking under the bush? What would you find there?'

'A dunnart, perhaps.'

'That's a rat …or mouse, isn't it?'

'To the uninformed, yes.' His tone was slightly acid. Resentful of anything he thought betrayed ignorance of the natural world? Or perhaps he felt she was sneering at him.

After a pause for a deep breath he continued in a more measured, pedagogical manner. 'The dunnart is a tiny marsupial known to use the lower leaves of the yacca for shelter. That is very important for its survival. The problem is that, as yacca plants are removed by farmers, there are less sheltering places for the dunnart and over the years their population shrinks. This island dunnart is different from others on the mainland.' His voice then took on a little quiver, emotion taking hold again. 'It's unique to this island and people are wiping it out!'

'Yes, yes …' Pansy infused her voice with a gentle sadness. It was not false, but knowingly done: her intention was to side with his feelings. 'You're very fond of these little creatures, aren't you Arthur?'

'If people could come to know them better I'm sure they'd be fond of them too.'

'Well, first we need to know they are not just rats. Right?' She gave him a wistful smile.

He nodded. His face was more relaxed now. He seemed to be open to conversation and Pansy wanted to know more about him and his background. What drove the man?

She sat on the ground. 'What is it you want to achieve, Arthur? You know — with your campaign on the island.'

He cautiously joined her on the ground. It was obviously working. She tried not to look directly at him for long, which was very difficult for her.

He explained at some length how he wanted to make Kangaroo Island one vast educational site, where native species could be fully protected from predation and exploitation by humans, where children and adults could come for expeditions guided by experts to learn firsthand about the natural world of Australia. He mentioned particular species as examples — wallabies, goannas and skinks, black cockatoos and blue fairy wrens — and explained their characteristics. 'I know the government says it protects *some* of the island.' And then with more heat he added, 'but it's not much, and people often break the rules and get away with it!'

Pansy listened closely. His ideas were based on deep scientific knowledge and his ideals burnt fiercely. 'You have a very clear picture of what it could be like — a huge school for the state, eh?'

He leapt to his feet. 'No! For the whole *world*, Pansy! The world!'

'Ah! Yes.' She noted the flicker of a smile about his lips and responded with her own. It was time to probe gently into his personal life. Still sitting, she picked up a stick and drew idle lines in the dust. 'I know Miss Crump and Kenneth Maine have a similar interest in the island. But do others in Adelaide agree with you,

79

Arthur? We don't hear everything from across Backstairs Passage.'

He mentioned a few names she had never heard before. He said they were trying to persuade parliamentarians of the value of the plan.

'But they all sound like university people, Arthur. Politicians need to know the mass of *ordinary* people with less education will still vote for them if they turn the whole of Kangaroo Island into a reserve for native plants and animals. That's where the campaign has to concentrate, don't you think?'

His lips tightened. There was the hint of a twitch in an arm. But he nodded and said through gritted teeth, 'Perhaps so.'

She knew it was time for the next step. 'For instance, people you know well ... like your family. How do they see your plan?' Still keeping her eyes to the ground, she focussed on the lazy lines her stick drew.

He was still standing. 'Family?' Feet shuffled. He blew a hiss of air. 'I doubt whether they see it at all!'

'Do you mean they don't understand, Arthur?'

'Understand! They don't even listen ... or didn't ...'

She waited in silence, confident now that he would continue the conversation, even though he had begun to pace in that slow jerky way around several yaccas.

He returned to her and stood still, frowning as he spoke. 'It's been a long time since I talked to my family. In Adelaide I spend most of my time at the university and then go home to my own lodgings. They have their businesses and rowing regattas and debutante balls ... and they just laugh at me.'

'Oh! That's a shame, Arthur.'

Pansy let him go on at his own pace for some minutes. He did so now without prompting or encouragement, and eventually she formed a broad picture of this young man's life. Such a sad story.

Chapter 10

James Pearce was sweeping the dust off the veranda of his store at eight o'clock in the morning. It was one of the daily rituals that gave him comfort, reinforcing his personal fortress against the troubles and threats that snarled from the newspapers. Breakfast reading had presented reports of tensions between European nations; some authoritative people declared these signified the approach of an inevitable war, which would embroil Australia as part of the British Empire.

The faint sound of a motor penetrated his fortress. A boat? Some sort of machine? It grew louder. A loud babble of voices erupted in the street. James stopped sweeping and turned his eyes uphill to see what was happening.

A vehicle approached on the road. Why would that cause such yelling? This was no charabanc such as brought large groups of tourists to visit. This was a small motorcar meant to carry four or five. These vehicles almost never came to the island, and even then did not generate excitement like this. Faces of passengers were visible now, and the driver ... James stared and then gritted his teeth.

'Pamela!' Her name flew from his throat in a harsh whisper as his daughter passed. She sat boldly holding the steering wheel.

As if in reply, the car's horn blared and a pedestrian jumped back off the road.

Pansy did not notice her father; her attention was utterly on the road ahead, the pedals at her feet and the demands of the steering. She kept mentally flicking back to her sole driving lesson a few days ago, recalling Gerald's instructions as to when to use each handle, knob, pedal or thingamajig. Her heart was beating fast but the car seemed to be doing what she intended. Her passengers certainly seemed quite at ease, their chitchat flowing freely.

It had all happened completely by accident. She was walking away from the Ocean View Hotel after delivering a basket of buns the management had ordered. She recognised Gerald the chauffeur on the driveway as she passed. His face was contorted and he was clutching his belly. She went to him.

'Gerald! What's the matter?'

'Pansy!' He winced. 'Afraid I'm ill, old girl. Came on very suddenly, you see, and they ...' He jerked his thumb to indicate a group of suited men some yards to his rear. 'They *must* have a driver to go to their meetings. We did have another bloke, but he went off to deal with some other business before my stomach started to play up.'

'Is there no one in the hotel who could drive?'

'Not at the moment.'

She thought for a moment. 'Well, there's me.'

'Eh?' He stared at her. 'Well, I believe you could drive it … but no, Pansy. You don't have a driver's license. They wouldn't hear of riding with an unlicensed chauffeur, no matter how much I vouched for your ability.'

'Well, Gerald, guess what!' Pansy chortled, excitement kindling inside her. 'I *do* have a license. Not with me, but it's certainly at home. Do they have time for me to fetch it?'

'*You* have a license? How on earth …?' He stared again for a second before twisting in pain again. 'Anyway, you're a woman.'

'You know there are many ladies driving cars in Adelaide! Talk to them, Gerald!'

With a groan he staggered two steps and dropped heavily into a chair. 'If they leave in about twenty minutes they should reach their meeting on time. I'll try to talk them into it. Get your licence.'

People along the main street swapped smirks and chuckles when they saw Pansy Pearce sprinting downhill along the main street, skirt hem held up to let her knees thrust toward the sun. James Pearce's gaze was torn from his newspaper to his daughter's stormy rampage between front door and office. The street watchers then guffawed as heartily as kookaburras when the lanky lass sprinted back uphill, skirt flapping from her pumping fists, and did not stop until she reached the steps of the Ocean View Hotel.

'The craziest ratbag on the island!' They all agreed.

Battling his stomach pain, Gerald held up the license she brought from the house and managed to introduce Miss Pearce to Mr Homburg and Mr Butler. 'I have observed her driving ability when she … ah …

helped me test the car. Gentlemen, I am sure you will be in safe hands if you allow her to be your chauffeur.'

He pulled her aside and murmured to her. 'It's a short drive and the road's good. I know you can do it, old girl. Just keep the speed down. And thank you for doing this.' He hurried away to his room, face pale.

Pansy's license had arrived only yesterday. After the driving lesson with Gerald, Pansy had remembered that her father long ago had obtained an official form with the intention of applying for a driver's license. 'A motorcar,' he said, 'might be an excellent asset for our business.' After a while the idea lost its shine for him and the form lay forgotten on a shelf of the office desk. So Pansy grabbed it, filled in the required details and sent it with payment to the Registrar of Motor Vehicles in Adelaide.

Should she now be glad she had done it? Behind the wheel of the Maxwell she was not sure. The motorcar moved along nicely and the government Ministers seemed content, but the impulse that got her this role also led to absence from her job. Connie Pincombe was on duty, a very capable waitress who could oversee the others as necessary. Passing the tearooms, a swift glance told Pansy the place had no customers at the veranda tables, and it was unlikely there were more than one or two inside at this early hour of the day.

Pansy drew a deep breath and released it with a smile. This was the most adventurous thing she had done for years. Possibilities, shapeless but alluring, could be felt waiting somewhere in her future. Gerald had said the meeting was to be held at Joe Benson's place. She turned off the main street and headed west, out of town.

'Well, well, Pansy!' Mrs Benson walked beside her behind the men as they left the Maxwell. 'You *are* a bag of surprises, aren't you? What do your parents have to say about you doing this?'

'I daresay I'll find out tonight—not that it makes one jot of difference.' She did her best to smile politely. 'I am of age, after all.'

It turned out to be more like a visit to a local resident than a meeting. There were several other settlers there on Benson's veranda, but Pansy counted eight people in all, apart from the ministers and herself. She sat on the periphery of the gathering and sipped Mrs Benson's tea. For some time, the visitors listened to the islanders talk about their farms and hopes.

Before long Benson began to raise issues of concern. 'The possums are a problem for some people, but since you lifted the ban on killing 'em gangs of men who don't own any property just wander everywhere to get thousands of skins. Trouble is, they've taken sheep and chooks and even clothes the missus put out on the line.'

And naïve girls, thought Pansy, considering a mental image of Jenny and the man at the tearooms.

'And this has been happening on other properties too?' Mr Butler looked around the group.

A chorus of affirmative noises responded.

Benson spoke again. 'I've had to chase one of them off a few times—big bloke, and aggressive he is. I don't want it to come to a fight. So we reckon you should make possum hunting illegal without a license, and give the licenses only to property owners or those they nominate.'

The two ministers agreed to take the idea back to Adelaide for serious consideration. They asked a few questions about the general needs of farmers and islanders.

'Roads,' Benson grunted. 'We need more and better. If we can get roads going to closer points on the coast where ships can load, it would make the gumming much more profitable. Then we could clear more land and do it faster. Then we could produce much more food and wool for you people in Adelaide. Just give us the roads!'

Others chimed in. 'And the roads are getting churned up!'

'The drays have been carting more and more yacca gum to the ships over the last few months,' Benson explained. 'Often they need a team of six horses.'

Mr Homburg leaned forward. 'Joe, did you know that the work of six of those drays can be done by one,' he held up a finger, '*just one* motor lorry?'

There was silence for a moment. The radical notion was obviously a shock to the minds met here.

Joe Benson cleared his throat. 'One more thing, gentlemen. There are certain people pushing hard for Kangaroo Island to be made a reserve. Then land can't be cleared and pests can't be killed. That would destroy productive farming here, farming that supplies you people in the city with the essential food you need. I hope you will see these people as the fools they are.'

The two ministers said vague things about looking sensibly at all proposals. Little more was said, save random chatter.

With all the party seated in the car once again, Mr Butler asked Pansy to return them to the hotel, where they would receive several deputations during the day.

'Certainly,' she said. But when the motor leapt to life it seemed to trigger a brilliant idea in her mind. She turned to the men in the back seat. 'Gentlemen, if you have some time to spare would you do me the honour of enjoying morning tea in Mrs Harding's Tearooms?'

'Oh, yes please! What a grand idea, Miss Pearce!' They hungered aloud for scones with jam and cream. She smiled to herself between bumps on the corrugated road. At least she could say to her employer that her absence from duty was part of a plan to bring two of the most important men in South Australia to her establishment.

She called over her shoulder. 'Gentlemen, if you would like to have a photographic souvenir of your stay on the island, I could send for a man in our town who does an excellent job with a camera. Would that be to your liking?'

Again they agreed readily. Such photographs could always be used to show their constituents what sterling efforts the pair made for the betterment of the state. And another grin broke out on Pansy's face as she imagined how pictures of these highly placed men at morning tea could embellish Mrs Harding's advertisements for the tearooms.

So her morning would appear to be devoted to the business, after all. With a deep sigh of satisfaction, Pansy hummed to herself. Mrs Harding would certainly hear about this triumph on her return.

Another day at the tearooms had drawn to an end. Summer's heat was gone for a while, nudged aside by a little cool breeze from the Southern Ocean on the other side of the island. It was just strong enough to ripple the surface of the pond. Reflected sunlight sprinkled into the balmy air. Pansy stood back from the pond to take in the scene.

Connie needed to do some shopping after work, so Pansy had volunteered to collect little Benny and bring him home. Mrs Dodd told her Amy had taken him here for a walk.

In Amy's arms, Benny curled his fingers around a leaf on a gum tree, then around some pendant she-oak foliage. Amy took him to a mass of correa blossom and let him explore the little pink and white bells. The pair looked so content, so intimately part of this serene spot, that Pansy did not want to disturb them. She stood back and watched, partly concealed by bushes.

It was not long before Amy looked up and saw her. A brilliant smile lit her face. The dancing light from the pond caught her eyes for an instant, and they shone bright honey brown.

She stood the little boy on the ground and held his hands. 'Look, Benny! Who's that? Walk to Pansy now. Call him, Pansy. Call him!' The child took a wobbly step, then another. 'Good boy! You're learning fast ...'

Pansy stepped a little closer and held her hands out. When he reached her she picked him up, raised him high above her head and cried, 'Hurray!'

They sat on a rocky outcrop and let him spend a little time exploring the spot. The ground was quite level just there, and clear enough for him to be safe. Amy opened her bag and, bringing out the ever

89

present sketch pad, set to work with a focus on the yaccas growing in several clusters around the pond.

'You and your mum have enjoyed minding him, haven't you?' Pansy watched her while keeping one eye on the child, who examined another leaf in his chubby hand. 'Mrs Harding comes back tomorrow. I'll ask her to make Connie a fulltime employee. Then she should make enough money to pay you two for your services.'

'You sound sure it will happen.'

'I'm confident. Connie saved us from disaster a few times when crowds of visitors came through the doors without any warning. She's good at her job and without her we could never have served them. I'll point that out to Mrs Harding. And my opinion pulls some weight with Mrs Harding these days.'

'Mum and I won't be asking for much—the pleasure we get from having Benny is enough really. The important thing is that Connie gets to keep her boy.'

Amy's hand moved briskly on her pad. Occasionally she fixed her gaze on the tall yacca close by, which now began to take shape on the paper. Benny played, making contented little noises to himself. A pair of magpies burst into song in a tree overhead; their brilliant carolling rolled through calm air and over the peaceful surface of the pond. All this was like a sponge that absorbed time. Pansy sat on the rock, feeling more confident than she had for a long time that her life was on the right track. Optimism seemed to shine from every part of the scene.

A small choking sound tore her from her reverie. 'Benny!' Pansy leapt to her feet and rushed to where he sat, pale and retching. Leaves protruding from his mouth told the story. Between his crying and belly heaves, she cleared his mouth with one finger. The problem solved, he quietened and wanted to walk again. She lifted him to his feet and let him hold her fingers as he tottered to the water's edge. The ground sloped very gently into the pond, so she removed his shoes and let him paddle. Then he sat at the water's edge.

Amy's voice was sudden and urgent. 'Just keep him there for a moment! Yes, let him sit while I sketch him.' After two minutes she held her pad out at arm's length and studied her work.

'Yep, that'll do.' She rose and gathered her belongings.

They headed back to town, singing nursery rhymes while the little boy bounced and giggled on Pansy's shoulders.

Chapter 11

Mrs Harding smiled as she poured tea into two cups. 'Yes, it was a grand time in Adelaide. The weather was much hotter there, of course, and everyone I spoke to kept saying they'd heard what a corker mild climate we have here on Kangaroo Island. The word is certainly spreading, Pansy! We'll have more and more coming here for holidays. And there's news of another plan to establish a health sanatorium here.' She offered the milk jug to Pansy. 'All good prospects for our business here, eh?'

Our business! Pansy's heart beat faster at the implication of shared ownership. Was the proposal about to be made?

Mrs Harding leant back in her chair and sipped her tea. 'So now, old girl, tell me how things have been in my absence.'

Pansy gave her report of business during the owner's absence, occasional praise voiced by customers, how she had managed minor problems like broken crockery and a waitress giving the wrong amount of change to customers.

'I've heard something strange—something about you driving a motorcar through town, dear. Fiction, surely?'

'I did drive it, Mrs Harding.' Before the listener's frown could lead to words, she leapt in to narrate in detail how it was part of a plan to host the two government ministers for morning tea. 'We can use that visit as a valuable advertisement for our tearooms, Mrs Harding!' She paused and sat forward to make an impact. 'An important recommendation I would make is that you correspond with the Tourist Bureau about our need for more notice of their groups coming through. It was almost impossible to meet the demand sometimes when a charabanc arrived with a crowd. Luckily, I had an extra waitress on duty … which brings me to an important matter.'

Mrs Harding folded her hands on the table and raised her eyebrows.

Pansy drew a deep breath, aware that the eyes of her silent employer were trained coolly on her. 'You'll remember Connie Pincombe. She was a waitress here for quite a while. She did a very good job.'

Pansy recounted the story of how she had dealt with Connie's predicament. 'I knew I didn't really have the authority to take on a new employee, but it was an emergency and I only gave her part time work. She's very efficient and always pleasant with the customers. And she was a godsend, as things turned out, when those sudden arrivals of visitors took us by surprise.'

Mrs Harding's gaze was unwavering. She said not a word. What was she thinking?

'I would like to ask you to consider a further step, Mrs Harding.' Pansy drew breath again and sat forward. 'Connie really needs more than part time income to make a decent life for Benny and herself. I must tell you that Jenny behaved just as you suspected she would ...' Pansy set out the details of the other girl's negligence. 'I think our business will benefit if you make Connie fulltime and cut Jenny's time — or even dismiss her, if you see fit.'

A host of gulls released a cacophony of scraping squeals. Some circled high overhead, while others swooped and bickered on the wharf, drawn by a load of fish two men hauled from their boat. On the other side of the wharf a ship was ready for departure. The air was still and humid. Dark clouds presaged rain.

Near the gangplank three young women stood — Amy and Pansy both facing Connie Pincombe. Beside her was a large case. She was sobbing softly.

'I'm so, so sorry it came to this.' Pansy put her arms around the young woman. 'But I will never forget you and I most certainly won't forget little Benny! This is an injustice that must be set right.'

'Oh Pansy! What more can you do? The government people are in control. It's all my fault ...'

'You must never say that again, Connie! Do *not* let the world mould you into a self-blaming spineless creature as it would like.' She held the other's shoulders and looked intensely into her eyes. 'I *will* find ways to help, one way or another. Believe me, this is not the end.'

For a while, no more words were spoken. Amid the noise of the gulls Pansy reflected on the turn of events in recent days. Things had not gone the way she had anticipated. Mrs Harding, after listening very attentively to her proposition, had taken almost no time to reject it.

'I disagree with this idea. Jenny's attitude, in my opinion, is mainly due to immaturity. She'll become a good waitress with firm supervision and encouragement. Connie Pincombe, experienced and mature though she may be, could well prove to be a liability. You know, Pansy, the women I employ have always been unmarried and childless. The lass is in a real pickle, of course, but this business does not exist to compensate for the errors people make in their private lives.'

It was alarming to see how quickly Connie lost her meagre income, and it was only a matter of days before the police stepped in again, this time the sergeant himself conducting the investigation. Once more Pansy faced him.

'Connie has the support of two people who are willing to mind Benny whenever necessary. She just needs a little time to find a paying job — laundering, ironing, cleaning houses …'

Sergeant Lawrence obviously felt quite sure of his ground now. He shook his head. 'I'm sorry, Miss Pearce. I must proceed.' His tone was level, his words unhesitant. 'A lady from Adelaide will be coming to collect the child and take him to the children's home. It's for the best in the long term, I assure you.'

Pansy felt helpless as matters proceeded. The agonised separation of Benny from his mother on the wharf wrought tears from Amy and Mary Dodd as they kissed the little boy for the last time and held Connie's shaking shoulders. Pansy, granted leave by Mrs Harding for the occasion, did what she could to comfort them all. The ship moved out onto the ocean and dwindled to a speck on the horizon, leaving its pall of black smoke on the still air. There was a cavernous sense of the killing of hope, and anger burned deep within Pansy.

Now, she was on the wharf for the second time in a few days to farewell Connie, who herself had decided to move to Adelaide. To Pansy, self-blame was obvious in Connie's demeanour and the few words she uttered. 'No, Connie, it's not your fault you're in this situation. Never let yourself think like that.'

An officer called for all passengers to board. Connie picked up her case and turned to go, but Pansy restrained her. 'Look, Connie, take this.' She shoved an envelope into the dejected woman's pocket. 'Just a little money we put together to help you get started in the city. No, don't say anything! Now go. God bless — and make sure you write to me!'

Chapter 12

'I've finished two dozen—no, it might be closer to twenty-six.' Amy sat on a little wooden chair to survey the artworks spread around the room. Several hung on a wall but most stood on the floor, leaning against walls and the rough paint-smeared bench. 'I really want to have this one finished, though.'

Pansy studied the painting on the easel. A bush scene—mottled eucalypt trunks, she-oak foliage drooping, low shrubs and yacca bushes around a misty pond—explored by fingers of sunlight coming from a low angle.

She pointed to an unpainted area. 'You're going to put something different there?'

Amy did not answer. A faraway expression ruled her face. The silence, the half-open mouth, and the dwindled pupils all took Pansy back to the days in the little stone building when Miss Gibson would stand in front of the little girl seated at the school desk.

'You can hear me, Amy. I know you can. Now answer ... no, don't draw! Look at me!'

At times like this she would snatch the pencils from Amy and put them on her big teacher's desk on the higher floor at the front of the room.

'See, Amy? I will keep them there unless you earn the privilege of having them again.' Then she would give the little girl one pencil at a time as she answered her questions or completed assigned writing.

'Three sixes? Yes, eighteen. See, you can do it! Here is your red pencil. Now seven sixes?'

Amy's eyes wandered from her drawing of orchids to the box on Miss Gibson's desk. 'Please Miss, may I have the purple one? I need it for this flower.'

'Yes, I'll let you have the purple pencil—*if* you show me you have learnt your six times table. Now are you listening, Amy? Seven sixes?'

One by one the pencils would return to Amy's desk. It happened every school day for a long time. The strategy worked in that Amy demonstrated she could speak and read and write the things the education system stipulated she must.

Now and then the teacher would produce a large black box and place it ostentatiously on her desk. 'Today, Amy, I want you to do your very best in our weekly tests. If your results are good enough, I'll let you have the black box for fifteen minutes.'

Amy usually earned the reward. A few minutes before lunch or towards the end of the day, Miss Gibson would ceremoniously unlock the black box and place it on the girl's desk. It contained a large set of pencils whose colours were far more varied than those normally available to most children. Four shades of purple. Magenta, vermilion, ochres, turquoise. The little girl's face lit up as she ran her fingers over the array. Those short periods with the special pencils were golden for Amy.

Pansy now gazed at the young woman sitting on that little chair, staring through the window. Would she have learnt to read, write and calculate at all if teachers had not forcibly stopped her from drawing?

The late summer light pooled like wild honey in Amy's dark eyes and spread a soft sheen over her brown cheeks. There had never been any pretence about her, yet she seemed to live mostly in a world others could not enter. Pansy felt a sudden yearning but dismissed it just as abruptly.

Amy turned her eyes from the window and focussed on the painting before her. With decisive speed, she picked up a brush, dipped it into paint and placed two tiny dabs on the canvas.

'Anyway,' Pansy said, 'whether that one's ready or not, you've obviously got plenty to put on show. I'll make a booking for the town hall tomorrow. Now there are one or two things still to be decided. Who should be asked to formally open the exhibition? And exactly how many days should it last? And, Amy, have you thought about setting prices in case people ask to buy your work?'

Amy's wide eyes turned to her. 'Prices?'

'This is your first leap into the world of the professional artist. You must approach it in a professional manner!'

'I have no idea about prices.' Amy shook her head slowly. 'I've never thought about it.'

'If Margaret brings back good professional assessments of your work, I suppose you could ask for a pound or two apiece.'

Margaret had given an assurance, as she and Kenneth stood on the wharf before boarding the *Karatta* a few days earlier. 'I'll be seeing people highly regarded for their judgement on the quality of paintings in Adelaide.' She gestured to the two paintings by Amy she was taking with her to the city. 'When I show them these works I will ask for written statements of their opinions. If we can gather endorsements like that it will raise the stature of our exhibition in the public eye.' A sly wink came as she trod the gangplank. 'I will even approach Mr Hans Heysen!'

In the fading light of the studio, Pansy pulled her thoughts back to the present. She grasped Amy's slim shoulders and half whispered in excitement. 'My goodness, Amy! Just think. Heysen! Wouldn't *that* man's approval be worth something?' They had both read about the famous South Australian painter in the newspapers. 'With that sort of endorsement, I think you could ask for...' She shrugged. 'Two pounds? Does that sound right? Oh, I don't know! Make sure you talk with Margaret about it. She'll know what people will pay, I'm sure.' She heard the door handle turn. 'Oh hullo, Mr Dodd!'

Jack Dodd had always spent as few words as possible on her, but she never failed to observe at least the conventions of politeness with him. She faced him now to invite a response. His big frame filled the doorway. His skin was dark, darker than his daughter's, and darkened further perhaps by the scowl on his face. Lips stretched tight at the corners but did not manage to turn upward into the smile he half-heartedly tried to shape. With a tiny nod he was gone.

Pansy turned to Amy, eyebrows raised.

The younger girl met the silent request for explanation. 'Sorry. Foul mood lately.'

'Why?'

Amy shrugged. 'Trouble at work, probably. That's usually the problem when he gets like that.'

From another room came the voices of Amy's parents—his curt and hard, hers almost too quiet to hear. His feet trod heavy and swift. The front door opened and slammed behind him. The house pulled back the blanket of silence over itself. The incident hung in the back of Pansy's mind well beyond that afternoon.

She was relieved that Jack Dodd was absent when she visited the household again some days later. Mrs Dodd's offer of tea was very welcome.

With Amy, they sat in the kitchen on the shady side of the house. The window looked out into the backyard—a gum tree, a wattle, a bed of carrots and green vegetables, a trellis of beans. Here and there chooks clucked and pecked among the plants. The air drifting through the window was just pleasantly warm.

Pansy took a sip of her tea. 'Well, I've booked the hall. The show will run for four days beginning on a Friday.'

The other women nodded and eyed her over the rims of their teacups.

'So we have a little over two weeks to be ready. And I've had a letter from Margaret Crump. She'll be back here next week to stay until the exhibition has finished.'

That the letter had come to Pansy, rather than to Amy who was actually the principal artist in the exhibition, came as no surprise to the others. On first

101

meeting, people usually picked her as a strong organiser, especially in contrast to her retiring and gentle friend.

'And she sends excellent news.' Pansy paused for dramatic effect. 'The Tourist Bureau has agreed to put together holiday trips for visitors with our exhibition as a major item on the itinerary.'

Amy's eyes widened. Her mother chuckled.

'Yes, imagine the charabancs chugging into town every day! But there's more ...'

Margaret Crump had used her reputation and contacts well. Three prominent authorities on art had expressed very favourable opinions on viewing two paintings by Amy. They would provide letters of endorsement attesting to the emerging artist's outstanding ability which could be used in publicity.

Mrs Dodd put a pot of fresh tea on the table and motioned to them to help themselves.

Pansy continued. 'The lady is obviously highly connected. She's even managed to get an appointment to see Hans Heysen—just as she said!'

'Ah!' Amy's voice was very rarely so loud. 'Heysen!' She gazed to some invisible faraway spot.

The name jiggled a connection for Pansy. *Heysen*. Another German. And that brought to mind Mr Homburg, the Attorney General, her recent passenger in the Maxwell tourer. She had read in *The Register* about his family, also members of the large and longstanding German community of South Australia.

Amy's sweet murmur brought her back. 'I remember seeing some of his work in the Art Gallery when we visited Adelaide years ago. Those big red gums, the misty hills—all so beautiful.' Her gaze came back to Pansy, then her mother. 'I could never be as good as that!'

Pansy's retort was instantaneous. 'Of course you could! I bet he writes a great assessment. You wait and see!'

The sound of heavy footsteps coming through the front door brought a hush to the kitchen. The three women listened as Jack Dodd stomped about the house. Pansy knew he would be anxious to get to the pub. After some splashing of water and more stomping, the front door banged shut.

Amy and her mother drew deep slow breaths, exhaled and sat back in their chairs.

'Good.' Mary Dodd's voice was only a whisper.

'At least he didn't come out here.' Amy's words were muttered, her face taut.

Her mother noticed Pansy studying their faces. 'I'm sorry, Pansy. He's been pretty bad tempered lately. Well, worse than usual, shall we say? Likely to go crook about anything.'

"Oh yes, Amy mentioned that.' The right time to probe the matter, she felt, but the question had to be casual. She kept her eyes fixed on the teapot, pouring tea as she spoke. 'Has he often been that way, Mrs Dodd?'

The answer was a sigh, then a moment's silence as Pansy watched her teaspoon stirring in her cup. 'Well, they say men get crotchety when they get older. But he's always been a man's man—you know, out with the boys for sport and cards and all that ...'

Amy's voice jumped in. 'He's never had time for me and he treats you as his slave.' A steel-edged, harsh voice.

Pansy was shocked. She had never heard Amy speak like that before. Her mother said nothing. She smoothed the table cloth in long, slow sweeps of one hand, as though she were soothing herself.

After a few seconds that seemed like an hour, Mrs Dodd heaved another long sigh. 'Odd how things come back into your head as you get older. You know, things from long, long ago.' She rubbed her eyes with both dark hands. 'I keep thinking of my Aunty Lizzy.'

Amy stared at her. 'Who's that? I've never heard of her before.'

'Haven't seen her for years and years ...wonder if she's still alive somewhere ...' Mrs Dodd stared through the window to some distant invisible point. The gentle clucking of the chooks in the garden drifted to the kitchen table.

The others waited for her to say more, but Amy soon gave up. She slapped her hand on the table. 'Mum! Who is Aunty Lizzy?'

In both speech and gesture Amy was asserting herself to a degree Pansy had never known. This was fascinating.

'Oh ...' Mrs Dodd blinked twice and glanced at Pansy and then her daughter as if they had suddenly appeared from nowhere. 'She was ... well, I was taught to call her *Aunty*, but I think she could have been my cousin really ... quite a lot older than me, she was ...'

She was starting to fade away again. Amy slapped the table again, more gently this time. 'Your cousin, Mum?'

'Yes, well, I grew up with her around all the time, you know. We were really pretty close, used to go out bush to trap wallabies together and all that.' She nodded. 'Yep, taught me a lot, she did.' She eyed something invisible again.

'So, Mum, where would she be living, do you think?'

Mrs Dodd pulled herself back again. 'Oh … she'd be somewhere in the bush, I reckon, probably a bit to the west. That's where she always took me when we camped out.' She massaged her eyes. 'Yeah, I'd like to see her again.'

Pansy saw that shadows had taken over the garden. She stood. 'Time I went home.'

Amy went with her to the front door and they stepped out together. At the picket gate Pansy stopped and faced her. 'You seemed very keen to find out about your mother's aunty.'

'Well, I want to know about the family history. They've never told us much at all. She drops, you know, only snippets—and even then she won't finish what she's saying and you can never put it all together to make any sense. Dad won't say a word, of course.'

Pansy studied her face, its brown deepened by the gathering dusk. She saw the frustrated longing there.

Amy met her gaze. 'You know what people whisper about us. I just want to know where I came from, who I am.'

Pansy did not give voice the resounding question in her mind. *And who, what am I?*

Over the next few days Pansy did her best to be effective at the tearooms while aware that her status had changed in Mrs Harding's eyes. No longer was there a comfortable assurance of becoming manager in due course; this would need some quiet contemplation before long. Right now, though, she was also thinking about arrangements for the art exhibition. It still needed to be opened by some dignitary. Reliable persons must be found who could supervise the hall while she herself was at work. If buyers for paintings appeared, who would ensure the purchase was made correctly and the payment kept securely?

An idea came to her. If she could show Mrs Harding that the event would bring a sizeable increase in visitors to the town—visitors who could be courteously advised to visit the tearooms and bakery—would she perhaps grant Pansy some leave from work to supervise in the hall?

Her attention was demanded from another direction too. Arthur Brewster-Leigh's continuing presence in the town and its environs sparked more incidents in the street. Drinkers outside the pub again taunted him as he passed by and two of them persevered to the extent of following him back to the boarding house where he lodged. Their shouted obscenities from beneath his window so upset the lady owner of the place that she sent her son to call the police. News of this reached Pansy's ears and she dropped into the boarding house to see how Arthur was dealing with his situation.

'He's out,' said the owner of the house, a plain-speaking widow who had lived on the island all her life. 'Know a bit about him, do you?' Her tone said *I wish I didn't.*

'We've spent some time chatting. He's an unusual man, but he means no harm. Some people are just too quick to condemn him.'

'Huh! He goes out of his way to avoid chatting *with me*! But he must've said enough to other people to make them go crook. Mad as cut snakes, they were!'

'It takes a little time to understand him …'

'Listen, Miss Pearce, I don't need to *understand* my guests. If they pay regular and go by house rules, I'm happy. But when they start fights outside and bring them back here, that's when they wear out their welcome. So please have another of your little *chats* with Mr Brewster-Leigh and tell 'im there'll be no lodging here if we have any more of this.' And she opened the door to usher the visitor out.

Pansy spied Arthur the next day as he returned from one of his expeditions into the bush. His shirt hung out and dirt smeared his trousers. Through spectacles he examined an open notebook as he walked. He almost collided with her.

'What did you find today?'

He looked back to his notebook. 'Very many species in a small area.'

Seeing he was again lost in thought, she decided to speak bluntly. 'Arthur, you must be more careful to avoid disputes with people in town. The way you're going you'll be kicked out of the boarding house and the police are likely to ask you to move on. I don't want that to happen.'

His thin high voice flew into the air and his arms gesticulated wildly. 'They just yell names as soon as they see me!' He kicked at a rock. 'I try to say nothing and keep walking but then they follow me!' His shoulders jerked violently.

His tantrum continued. Pansy stayed at his side, avoiding eye contact to help him keep talking.

'It was the same at school. They'd just keep it going, no matter what I did. Throwing words, then pushing and tripping ...'

It all flowed out then. They walked for some time, he talking, she only occasionally uttering a word or

107

two to encourage him. She suspected some of the memories he poured out had been buried for years, perhaps never told to another person until now. By the time they parted outside Arthur's lodgings, Pansy had a vivid picture of his life and how he saw it.

'Honestly,' she declared the next day to Margaret Crump, who had returned. 'I've tried to keep him out of trouble whenever I could, but trouble shadows him!'

They agreed to corner Arthur at the earliest opportunity and have an earnest discussion with him about his situation on the island. Then, sitting in the Dodds' kitchen with Amy and her mother, they turned to the matter of the coming exhibition.

'Well now, ladies, have I got something to show you!' She extracted an envelope from the depths of her handbag and, with a grand flourish, laid it on the table. 'Allow me to deliver this letter from Mr Hans Heysen himself.' She faced Amy squarely. 'He assured me that it states precisely the opinion of your work that he told me in person. You are on your way, my girl!'

Amy stared agape at the envelope lying before her.

'Well, go on—open it! Read it!' The others wriggled and clapped with excitement.

'Amy, if you don't I will.' Pansy drummed the tabletop. 'You have three seconds …'

The Heysen letter was a glowing endorsement. It told of superb composition and technique, outstanding use of colour to convey mood, and a wonderful eye for detail. And it was not the only document in the Crump armoury. Two authoritative academics had also written glowing praises and encouragement for Miss

Dodd, "the Kangaroo Island painter with a naïve and exciting talent". All added up to a trove of very persuasive appraisals which could be quoted in newspaper advertisements, or posters and leaflets to attract people to the exhibition and encourage them to purchase Amy's work.

'So now, Amy,' proclaimed Margaret Crump, 'we must think about preparations for your debut!'

Chapter 13

The Kangaroo Island summer drifted into February. Paintings were finished and named. Margaret helped Amy stretch and mount them; some she put into frames brought with her from Adelaide. Together they planned how to place the works in the town hall.

Pansy looked in one evening and found Amy admiring a newspaper advertisement for the exhibition. She curled the page over to see the banner. 'Ah, *The Register*, eh?'

'Yes, and Margaret has it appearing in *The Advertiser* and *The Observer* and ... I forget the others. The Tourist Bureau is arranging more publicity too ...' Her voice trailed away. She stared through the window into the distance.

'What are you thinking about?'

Amy took a few seconds to make a barely articulated reply. 'Mmm? Oh, ah ... Lizzy.'

Pansy sifted her memory. Lizzy? Yes, she remembered, the woman Mary Dodd had talked about, the relative who had taken her under her wing when she was very young.

'What about her?'

Amy drifted back from her rumination. 'Well, I thought I'd try to find her.'

'Why?'

'Mum would love to see her again. And I would love to know her. She might tell me about our family — who they were, where they came from.'

Reflecting on the ignorance and longing that Amy expressed, Pansy was grateful for the memory she had of her own grandparents. In hindsight, those school holiday periods spent with them in Adelaide were intervals of bliss. The shopping days in Rundle Street, long picnics in the Botanic Gardens, building sandcastles on the beach at Glenelg, the unhurried Yorkshire chatter and chuckles of the doting old pair — all these recollections formed an inner pool of warm assurance that, despite her father, she was a creature of love.

Oh, if only Amy could one day have that satisfaction. But what if her search led to knowledge that was unwelcome? Would she wish for the fog of ignorance to return?

Such musings meandered through the morning in the quiet tearooms as Pansy moved from one table to another, here polishing a sugar bowl, there shifting an ashtray. The air was hotter than on recent days. Outside the building all seemed especially calm, not a single person or horse in the main street. No customers had appeared since opening.

Mrs Harding brought a teapot and cups from the kitchen to the veranda deck and placed it on a table. 'We might as well sit down for a cuppa.'

Pansy joined her. Further up the hill a flock of black cockatoos rasped in chorus as lazy strokes of

111

their wings carried them across the green-grey tops of the gumtrees. Downhill, in the bay, sea and sky met in unmoving azure of mutual admiration.

The muffled thud of distant hooves crept into the air. The sound grew. A horse galloped into town. The eyes of the two women met in a silent question. They watched the rider pass the tearooms, rein in at the police station, dismount and hurry inside.

Two minutes later the man emerged from the police station and remounted, to be joined by Sergeant Lawrence bringing his horse from the stable at the rear of the building. The two rode up the hill at a brisk trot and the drumming of hooves seeped away into the landscape.

'I'm sure we'll hear an interesting yarn about that before long.' Mrs Harding grunted as she rose from her seat and began to put the crockery onto a tray. She disappeared into her office.

Pansy brought a ledger onto the veranda, along with a little pile of receipts and scribbled notes, and immersed herself in book entries.

Soon she was interrupted by Amy's voice. 'Morning, Pansy. How about a pot of tea? I've got a bit of news!'

Propelled by hunger for understanding of her ancestry, and using as a guide the few remembered facts her mother could retrieve of the vicinity Lizzy once inhabited, Amy had saddled one of her father's horses and ridden out to find the mysterious relative. After several hours, a combination of instinct and random exploration brought her to a shack made from timber and corrugated iron. Looking at Pansy now, Amy shook her head. 'No one would see it unless they were searching for it. It's not far back from the sea, in

112

the middle of some thick scrub.' There, surrounded by dogs, sat a dark-skinned old woman who confirmed she was, in fact, Lizzy.

'She remembers Mum perfectly,' Amy said. 'She talked about things the two of them did when they were very young—before Mum was married—and she reckons she's actually Mum's aunty. She was really keen to know how Mum is going.' Amy's tone rang with amazement. But she paused at that point, interrupted by noise on the road.

The two women watched a man ride down the hill and into the main street. He went straight to the pub.

Amy sipped her tea thoughtfully. 'You know, the way Lizzy asked was odd.'

'Odd? How?'

'Well, as though she assumed Mum would be in a bad way. Once Mum and Dad were married Lizzy stayed away.' Amy's lips tightened and her eyes narrowed. A tension entered her voice. 'Didn't sound too keen on my father. Maybe that's why she kept away from Mum.' Again she paused as their heads turned back to the street.

The rider of the horse had run inside the pub. Now he returned to the street with several other men. They all ran in different directions. Soon there were groups of animated people in the street, talking loudly.

Pansy resumed the conversation. 'Did you ask Lizzy about meeting your mother again?'

'Yeah. She wants to. But she doesn't want to walk into town by herself.'

Pansy raised her eyebrows.

'It's not only that she's old,' murmured Amy. 'She's convinced people wouldn't welcome her in town.'

113

Pansy nodded. Lizzy was right; most people had little time for aborigines. 'Well, we could give her a ride, couldn't we? With us she'd be safe enough. And she'd only go to your house, so maybe no one would see her anyway.'

Amy smiled. 'That's just what I told her.'

Amy was pouring more tea when the loud tread of feet on the timber steps to the veranda announced the arrival of two women. They bustled over to the table where the friends sat.

Pansy leapt to her feet. 'Good morning, ladies. Please take any table.'

'Yes, thank you! Tea for two ... and scones please.' The customers were quite agitated. One grabbed a menu, fell back into a chair, and started fanning herself. The other put her head in her hands.

Pansy paused halfway to the kitchen. 'Is there something wrong, ladies?'

'Bad news!' The woman looked a little pale.

'Joe Benson has been murdered!' squeaked the other.

The sun's last rosy glimmer lingered over foliage around the clearing. The little boy's bare toes held the ground securely as his heels rose and his arms reached high. His fingers stretched out in urgent invitation. Then his hands cupped to receive. His heels returned to ground and he sank gently to sit. Eying the gift in his hands, he smiled.

'They say they're my family. They just have to wait till it's time.'

'There's nothing there!' The older boy thrust his finger to point at the little palms. 'Your hands are empty. You're stupid!'

'No one can see them till it's time. But they let me. They say I'm different …'

The bigger boy bent down and sneered into the beaming face. 'Yeah, different alright!' He pushed the little one savagely so that he rolled onto the leaf litter. 'Get up. It's time for tea, stupid.'

The small cupped hands rose and opened. 'Bye bye! See you tomorrow …'

He sprang to his feet and began to follow the older boy, but stopped abruptly and turned to face the three heads that towered over both of them, dusk now clotting their huge bristles with shadow. Hands at his sides and voice now smaller, he spoke in a reverent tone. 'Goodbye, Three-tree. I'll come again tomorrow.'

A puff of breeze rattled the bristles and then the clearing was empty and still.

Chapter 14

Amy had named the piece *Yacca and Child*. Pansy gazed at it. From all those hours, in which Amy had stared at the canvas, stroked paint on, stared for another few minutes, made dainty dabs of another colour, paced around with her eyes repeatedly reverting to the canvas, rushed to the easel and added another single slow streak; from all those hours of concentration a scene had emerged whose effect on people was powerful and profound. And she knew the child in the picture developed from Amy's sketches of little Benny by the pond.

Margaret Crump, the first viewer, had scanned it as one of a dozen or so other images and passed on, only to step back to it later and remain there, silent and still. After several minutes of contemplation, all she could say was, 'Astounding!' Afterwards she insisted on placing the painting at the centre of the exhibition, on a solitary easel, in a position that distinguished it from all other works hung on walls.

On opening day, the visitors admired all items, their discussions including little remarks in praise of various aspects of this one and that. But about *Yacca and Child* they said very little. Some viewers came to it and stood, unmoving and unspeaking, until it seemed they would never move on. Others would give it a few seconds of attention, proceed to other pictures and suddenly return to the one that apparently would not let them go.

Pansy stood near the door, collecting admission money, with Amy nearby to greet people and occasionally engage in discussion of her work.

'I'm sure you will feel like refreshments after inspecting our display,' Pansy said to the entering viewers. 'So I recommend Mrs Harding's Tearooms, just a little way up the hill. Excellent Devonshire teas. Buns and cakes to rival any of your city bakeries! Yes, madam, far better even than Balfour's!'

'Mrs Harding will think you're just the ant's pants once this mob walks into her place!' Amy giggled. 'You'll have an offer of promotion in no time.'

Pansy grunted. 'We'll see.' She said no more. She was unsure how Mrs Harding regarded her these days.

There were, of course, a few people clearly uninterested in any exhibits; they either wandered in off the street following others through idle curiosity, or were there merely to satisfy the wishes of friends or family. But, by and large, the pattern of response to Amy's artworks was full of admiration, with departing references to *Yacca and Child* that included words like *mystery*, *haunting* and *deep*.

They kept the exhibition open until seven o'clock for the first day, allowing local people to come in after work. Margaret stood in a corner of the hall from time to time, to assess the effect of the exhibition. Towards dusk she came over to the other two and gave her judgement in a quiet but definite way. 'Well, my dears, I think we can say this little project has been worthwhile.' She turned to Amy. 'And you, my girl, have taken your first big step towards a making a career in art. You are opening the eyes of Australians to the beauty — the *mysterious* beauty — of the land they live in. You could be the next Hans Heysen!'

Amy gave her usual quiet smile with downturned eyes, in the manner Pansy had found so endearing since they were children. Then the smile withered and she seemed to brace herself as she stared across the room.

Pansy followed her gaze. Mary and Jack Dodd had entered.

Margaret touched Amy on the shoulder. 'This exhibition should make your parents very proud of you.'

'My father has never looked at my work. Never been the slightest bit interested.' Amy gave a little snort. 'He's probably here just to appear to be doing the right thing.'

Several townspeople interrupted with congratulations to Amy. As they chattered politely Pansy watched Mary Dodd linger at each painting, a little smile leaping to her face now and then. She had often seen her daughter's works at home, Pansy knew, but still loved to look at them. Her husband, flashing his big public smile and nodding ostentatiously now and then to people, merely glanced at each painting and moved on.

But then he froze. Seeing him from one side, Pansy noted the new tightness in his jaw, the intensity of his focus. The hand by his hip began to twitch.

'Mary!' He was some yards from his wife when he spoke. It was not a yell, not even loud — more of a vocal stab through the air. His wife stepped towards him without delay but he moved even more swiftly. Before she could be at his side he was on his way to the door.

Pansy saw the anger — mingled with fear, perhaps — in the glance he flashed at his daughter in passing. She saw the sudden pallor of his face as well. Amy saw none of this; her attention was still on her conversation.

What triggered this extraordinary behaviour? Pansy wandered thoughtfully across the hall to where Jack had stood immobilised a few seconds ago, and found herself confronting *Yacca and Child*. What was it about this picture that had caused such a stark change in Jack Dodd?

Pansy, work finished for the day, chatted amicably to Amy in the street. 'Yes, the tearooms had quite a few customers coming from the exhibition.' For what one would expect to be good news, the reply to Amy's enquiry sounded not at all happy. 'But that wasn't enough to help my prospects.'

'What do you mean?'

'Regular customers have complained about me to Mrs Harding. They object to the way I've supported the proposal to preserve large areas of bush across the island. They say it will ruin their lives ... stop their husbands from making money from farming, clearing their land ... that sort of thing.'

Of course, it was more than that. She described how her employer had pulled her aside and recited a

119

number of complaints; they included not only blatant support in public for stopping agriculture, but also associating with the 'unrespectable' Arthur, being involved in street brawls, interfering with police who were simply doing their duty in taking care of little Benny Pincombe. ...

Pansy raised upturned hands. 'And then she went into a whinge about how I employed ... how did she put it? *I employed an unneeded waitress without her authority.*' She rubbed her eyes in frustration, before mimicking Mrs Harding's aloof scolding tone. *'I don't know what has got into you lately, dear girl, but it has made me think again about your future in this business! I suggest you do some hard thinking about yourself.'* Pansy snorted. 'As if I haven't been doing that already!'

Seeing the sympathy on Amy's face, Pansy gave a wry grin. 'I don't know what to think. Everything's getting more and more ...'

A distant voice interrupted them. They turned to see Margaret Crump bustling towards them. She explained she had been on another bush walk with Gerald and Arthur when the sight of a group of yacca bushes reminded her of Amy's paintings.

'So I'd like to ask, Amy, if it's not too much trouble would you let me have another look at *Yacca and Child*? Something about it keeps buzzing around in the back of my mind.' She smiled at the young woman's instant nod and followed her inside the house.

Pansy watched a few minutes later as the lady stood before the picture. After a prolonged silent study, she asked to see other paintings in which yaccas appeared. 'Would you mind ... Oh, I do hope you don't mind my strange requests, Amy! But there is method in my madness, believe me. Would you please arrange these in the order they were painted?'

This done, Margaret spent another five minutes moving from one to the other and back again, step close to a piece and draw back. Now and then she would nod or shake her head. Waiting in silence without knowing why, Pansy grew restless, but curiosity would not allow her to leave. The lady finally drew herself erect and faced Amy.

'There's a distinct development of something in that series, isn't there?'

Amy frowned. 'I'm not sure I understand.'

'Well, sometimes it takes another pair of eyes to alert the artist to what she herself is expressing. I can't tell you precisely, my dear, but if you look at the way you've coloured the yacca leaves in each piece ... the light around the outside of the bushes ... I think you'll notice a progression. You're trying hard to tell the world something about these plants, aren't you? Or perhaps it's not so much about the plants themselves but something *around* them ...'

Amy shrugged with a slow shake of her head. 'Um ... you might be right. But I can't explain it.'

'Don't worry! Just keep painting and it will become clear one day.' Margaret looked again at *Yacca and Child*. 'Whatever it is, this piece is the closest you've come to the final revelation.'

Pansy stood outside the Dodd house facing the open doorway. Inside was Mary Dodd's face, diverse emotions flashing across it like fish in a pond. Surprise, of course, and happiness, but there was also something like uncertainty for a second; a trace of fear as she looked at Lizzy, the shadow in the open doorway against the bright daylight outside.

'Oh, Lizzy!' Mary was motionless at first and seemed unable to say another word. The two faced each other from ten feet apart, the one silent and the other giving a short soft belly chuckle.

Amy, outside the door, put an encouraging hand behind the old woman's shoulder. 'Well, in you go then — and then I can put the kettle on!'

Inside there was a fond embrace with a few muffled words from Lizzy and Mary before everyone moved to the kitchen. Amy set about making tea while the others sat around the table.

The journey that morning to Lizzy's shack had taken over an hour in the cart drawn by two strong horses, borrowed for the day. Amy and Pansy travelled the last few hundred yards on foot due to the density of the scrub. The wizened old woman sat on a chair beside her doorway, surrounded by half a dozen dogs. Once assured that they would visit only Mary Dodd, Lizzy agreed quite readily to accompany them.

Now in the Dodd kitchen, Pansy smiled and watched in anticipation. Would the mystery that hung over the history of this family — rarely, if ever, mentioned until recently — now be explained?

Mary broke the silence. 'So how fit are you, Lizzy? Still trapping the wallabies?'

'Gettin' a few now and then.' A hint of a grin threatened to crack the gnarled dark face of the older woman. 'Th' old legs are pretty stiff these days. But one of the farmers trades food for a wallaby sometimes, so I don't need to come to town.'

Another silence. At a steady but unhurried pace, Amy placed cups, saucers, spoons, sugar and milk on the table. She looked now at her mother, now at Lizzy, her eyebrows raised in expectation. Yet still the silence persisted.

Pansy noted tension in Lizzy's posture. And there was a repeated flicker of her eyes towards the kitchen door. Did she want to get out?

'Jack's out at work,' murmured Mary. 'Won't be back for hours.'

Lizzy eased back in her chair. Her eyes no longer glanced at the door. So that was it: she had been anxious about meeting Mary's husband and now, relaxed, she could eye the faces around her and finally gaze at Mary without wavering.

'Been a long time, but you don't look bad, Mary.'

'Yeah, crackin' hardy.'

'An' you've got a beautiful daughter. An' a son, she tells me.'

'Ted's working with his father just now. He's got a job in Adelaide to go back to soon. I dunno whether he will though.'

Their tongues loosening quickly, Lizzy and Mary tumbled into a sustained interchange of information about the past two decades and more of their separate lives. Then came reminiscences of shared youth. Smiles erupted into laughter, punctuated by moments of silent contemplation. Pansy had never seen Mary Dodd so enlivened; she seemed much, much younger. And Amy was clearly engrossed, her eyes scrutinising the two older women.

This continued for many minutes until Lizzy drew a deep breath and looked at Amy. 'You look like your mother, girl.'

'Yes, she does, doesn't she?' Mary put an arm around her daughter's shoulders. 'But she's a lot cleverer than her mother. Aren't you, love?'

Amy smiled and lowered her eyes.

Before she could say a word her mother continued. 'She did well at school. She reads books I can't understand. And she paints the most beautiful pictures, don't you Amy?'

Lizzy's attention seemed to intensify. She scrutinised the young woman's face.

'Yes,' Mary continued, 'Amy's paintings were up in the town hall for four days, and dozens and dozens of people came to see them. They even bought some!' She gave her daughter's shoulders a little squeeze.

Lizzy's gaze flickered between Mary and Amy. 'Could I see these paintings?'

Amy nodded. Everyone followed her to the room she used as a studio and watched her set out some of the works that had recently hung in the exhibition.

Lizzy stepped closer to look at each in turn. Three of the pieces featured yacca bushes. Each seemed to grasp the old lady's interest more than the others — especially the last. She stared at it for a few seconds, stepped back and stared for another few, and finally stepped very close to examine details.

Pansy saw that the painting was *Yacca and Child*. So it had won another devotee.

Lizzy turned to Amy. 'You got the knowing, eh girl?'

'Pardon me?'

Lizzy frowned as she looked steadily at the young woman. 'I can see it in them pictures. You *know*. You're like the old 'uns.'

Amy shook her head, uncertain. 'I … I'm sorry. I don't understand.'

Lizzy's mouth opened as if she was about to elaborate, but then she shot a fleeting glance at Pansy and her lips pursed. Her eyes swept over the array of paintings again. 'You're a very good painter, girl.'

Pansy pointed to the clock on a shelf and feigned surprise. 'Goodness me, look at the time! I need to go right now. It's been nice to meet you, Lizzy. See you again soon, everyone!'

She hurried out of the house. In the bright street she let her pace ease to a stroll. Amy would not have to take Lizzy home for a while yet. Time enough for the old woman, in the company of only female relatives, to feel free to divulge things Amy needed to know.

Before long a suitable moment would come for drawing it all out of Amy.

She could not go home, not yet, not with this maelstrom of voices and thoughts and feelings within her. She wandered onto a bush track that led along the coast, turned off along another track to wind through gums and she-oaks, and after who knew how long, found herself beside the pond. Weary, with an increasing ache of tension across her shoulders, she sat on a log.

What was happening? Just a few weeks back, life was straight forward and promising: twenty-three years old; a secure income with a managerial position almost certainly near; accepted by the island community as honest and intelligent, despite some half-hidden scoffing among old schoolmates. No confusion or major problems. How could all this collapse overnight?

No—perhaps not just a night. It started that morning just after the beginning of the year, when the little German appeared in the doorway, asking for horseshoes, scraps to use in making weapons, possibly for a war against her own country; and only two hours later she was herself at war against the unkind forces of her own country, which were bent on throwing a mother and her child to the dogs; and then came all the trouble over yacca. Yes, everything seemed to erupt from that morning onward. And now, here, she felt rejected, scorned, lost. The island, it seemed, had declared her an alien.

Her fingers stretched, wanting to hold something. Or someone. Yes, she longed to embrace someone, to let herself be immersed in intimacy, like dissolving in the pond that lay before her.

A pair of she-oaks let their hair hang each side of a yacca bush on the other side of the pond, shadowy and brooding. The full moon gleamed from the mirror of the pond. The brilliant pearls of a cheeky willy wagtail's song hung in the breathless air of evening. Everything seemed to be waiting.

How long she sat there she could not tell. But a little breeze suddenly rumpled the pond's surface and set the yacca leaves coruscating in the moonlight, and she felt she was returning from a sojourn outside time. She knew now what direction to take—wherever it might lead.

Chapter 15

Friday again. The horses fed and watered, Ted walked from the stables and stretched. The muscles in his hips and back were tight, the hard day clutching him still. Football fitness was way down after these weeks working on the island. Good thing Oskar Zoerner didn't know; he'd be scathing. Part of a normal working day with Zoerner's bakeries was to run around a set course and complete the number of exercises the boss stipulated. 'I'll give you a good steady job,' he said years ago when they met at a football match in Kingscote. '*If* you come over to Adelaide and train for our footy team—train the way I tell you.'

Ted stopped, bent to touch his toes and felt the hamstrings protest in both legs. 'It's time.' This weekend, on the beach, early, would be the start of his preparation for the 1913 football season. He would be in some sort of shape to resume life in Adelaide in … what, two weeks perhaps? Zoerner had said he could spare him until early March.

The thought of leaving his mother and sister behind worried him, though. Why? It wasn't that he needed them close for his own wellbeing; he was too independent for that now. He would just have to write to them often. And they could both come to Adelaide for two or three days now and then. Still, being separated by five or six hours on a steamship — that was a worry.

His father he could easily do without. He knew that now. These weeks of working for him and living with him had made it plain. The man whose word and ways were, years ago, the model of manliness to a boy had become something very different. Oh yes, he was still held in high regard by men on the island for his banter and physical toughness and ability to rally them in moments of need on the job, just as he had once been a hero for his achievements in footy and cricket. But at home with only his wife and two children that same man was very different.

That was it. That was the worry about his mother and sister.

The veranda of the pub was already occupied by at least a dozen men. The noise from inside was very loud; a lot of beer would be drunk this night. And there at the bar was his father, surrounded by his mates, flashing his grin and slapping backs. By the time the man got home he would be completely shickered.

'Hey, Ted! I'll get a schooner for you. Whadya think of 'im, boys? This 'ere's me son — champion half-forward for Norwood, thirty odd goals last season, took the best bloody marks in history. Blood oath 'e did! Here's your beer, lad. We'll drink to you!'

Ted sipped the schooner, grinned and nodded in appreciation as the other men raised their glasses to him and echoed his father's praise with a babble of references to football incidents.

His father wiped the foam from his face. 'Well, Ted, how many loads of gum did we pile up for the ship this week? Oh blimey, Charlie, she was a bloody hard week! But a couple more paddocks are cleared of yacca ... them drays never stopped ... this keeps up we'll need more drays 'n horses, I reckon ...'

Ted raised an eyebrow. 'You're getting lorries though—aren't you?'

The question was casual but the response stark. His father's dark eyes instantly narrowed and his jaw tightened. He turned away from Ted. 'Who told you that?'

'Oh, Uncle George was telling me about it a few weeks ago ...'

His father glared and his lips parted. Ted realized the mistake. He had revealed George had confided information with his nephew but kept the conversation secret from his brother, who was supposedly his business partner. And the man from Adelaide had spent some days with George recently— both shut in the office to make the plans for the expansion—without a word to Jack. Another strong sign, Ted realized, that his father was being sidelined.

Before any more could be said, a hand reached between them to tap his father's shoulder. 'G'day Jack ... you were askin' for me?' The voice was not familiar.

'Ah yeah, mate ... Jim! Good t' see you!' His father's face suddenly shone with carefree joviality again. 'How y' going? Hey, I'll shout you a beer!'

129

Ted recognised the man now — one of the pair of workers who had left the salt mine and pestered his father for a job some time ago.

The hand of Jack Dodd gave a hearty slap to the man's back. 'Listen, mate. I'm a bit desperate. We're busier than ever and I've just lost one of my blokes. You still want a job? Bloody good, Jim! You'll be cartin' yacca gum for a week or two. That should give you enough money to get on your feet and sail back to the city, eh?'

Ted saw the other man shake hands with him exuberantly before his father went on, his voice suddenly quieter. 'No worries, mate. Told you I'd keep you in mind, didn't I? But listen, Jim … mate, there's something special I want you to do …'

His father guided the man towards the exit, speaking confidentially into his ear as they went out onto the veranda. Why would a job offer be so secretive? And the team of carters had *not* lost a man: it was simply not true. So why did he go out of his way to hire this man?

Things seemed to be eating away at his father from the inside and he was doing his best to keep it hidden from the world. It wasn't only the behaviour he had just now witnessed. A few days back he had left his Uncle George's office after letting him know how much gum had been unloaded at the wharf that day. As he walked to his dray he glimpsed his father entering the office.

He sat holding the reins when an angry knot of aggressive men burst through the closed door. Both brothers were yelling but few words were distinct. 'Benson' was one he could make out. There was a repetitive bang that was probably Uncle George's hand hitting the desk—something he would often do for emphasis, only not quite as forcefully as this—and he was calling his younger brother names like 'stupid halfwit'. The replies, equally loud, reminded Ted of the loser's yelp in a dogfight. That was a disturbing voice, one he did not want to link with his father. A vague nausea made him swallow hard.

Now, as he left the last of his beer in the glass and quit the pub, the memory of that incident underscored the conclusion he had already reached. He needed to get away from his father. He strode across the road, slamming a fist into the palm of the other hand.

The early air was still. A gentle yellow sunlight slanted across the cove from the east as a pair of pelicans drifted on the flat sea, dipping beaks lazily for fish. Sand stretched for three furlongs to the rocky headland, firm and unbroken near the water's edge. Ted felt the invitation.

The first few paces were a little awkward but soon his calves began to loosen and a rhythm took hold. Trot for ten minutes or so. Some faster bursts later. *The body calls you to run. The trouble is most people don't listen.* Oskar Zoerner would say this to him often. *Don't be scared to be different from them, lad.* Ted pictured the older man striding out of his office in his waistcoat and pressed trousers to sprint past shoppers along the footpath of the Norwood Parade. *The small, still voice: always pay heed to your body, my boy.*

Ted wore only a pair of loose shorts. Muscles in his feet, constricted for weeks by work boots, stretched and flexed on the smooth damp sand. He realised that

131

despite his heavy breathing, a grin had broken out on his face. It was a relief to do this.

He reached the end of the beach, turned and headed back with the sun in his eyes. In the distance, near the water, was a tiny figure. A few seconds more and he knew the person was running towards him. At fifty yards he knew who it was. Completely unexpected; but momentary reflection told him he should not be surprised.

'Good morning, Ted!'

'G'day Pansy.'

They both halted. She stood facing him squarely, hands on hips. He almost laughed aloud at the sight.

'What's so funny?' She came a pace closer.

'Well, they're not exactly normal clothes you're wearing.'

She glanced down at the white divided skirt that ended well above her knees. 'Good linen, that is! Made them myself, just for running. What's the point of trying to run in clothes that stop you from taking a decent stride?'

'You do this often, then?' He was not really surprised. She did anything else women weren't supposed to do.

'When I can. First time I've seen you down here, though.'

'Been too long since my last run. Footy season starts soon. Gotta get back into form.'

'So you're going back to Adelaide, eh?'

He nodded. 'I haven't told anyone else yet. You'll keep it to yourself for a while, won't you?'

'Of course! Come on now. You mustn't stop your training. Can I run with you?'

He grinned again as they trotted. Who would have thought, back in his schooldays, that he'd be training on the beach with Pansy Pearce in their twenties? He and the other boys used to joke about how weird she was, and then in their teens how she was actually a man in disguise.

The trotting jolted her voice as she spoke now. 'You must be proud of your little sister.'

'Eh? Oh, yeah ... her paintings ... She made a tidy sum from the exhibition.'

'She has outstanding talent. If she sticks to it and learns more, there's no limit to how far she could go! Hans Heysen, watch out!'

'Well, I wouldn't know about that sort of thing. Looks as though she could earn some good money though.'

'Very different from Amy, aren't you Ted?'

He chuckled, but the trotting turned it into a series of grunts. 'Male and female ... of course!' Even as he said it the self-questioning began in his mind.

'Are they *that* different, Ted?'

He felt the conversation step into uncomfortable territory. He let out a loud guffaw, the easiest escape. 'Time for sprinting!'

Pumping his arms into a full swing, he shot ahead of her. There were almost a hundred yards of beach ahead. He wasn't the best in the football team over that distance, but not the worst either. He felt the strides lengthen as his knees lifted. This would soon bring the form back.

'Remember last time we did this?'

The shock of hearing her voice beside him was enough by itself to stop any answer, let alone the exertion of a full speed sprint. Her strides were

133

roughly in time with his but she had drawn level. Startled, he kept his gaze on the rocks ahead and maintained pace until he could feel drier and softer sand underfoot.

They came to a halt side by side and stood panting until there was enough breath to speak.

'I think I was about ten,' she said. 'You must have been about twelve.'

He said nothing, trying to recall the details.

She kept her eyes trained on his face. 'Across that paddock next to the school. Did I challenge you—or was it the other way around?'

He shook his head and shrugged; he could remember no such race. It must have been when nobody else was around to see it.

But she seemed to recall all manner of things. 'Just after that you started calling me *Pansy*. The little flower. Remember?'

'*I* did?'

'Too right.'

Somehow the name seemed to have always been there—no origin, no inventor. But perhaps what she said was true. The sense she was dominant in this conversation made him slightly uncomfortable. A few years ago he would have got away from her before any conversation could start. Even just a few weeks ago he was reluctant to face her. Yet now he wanted to linger, to be open to what she had to say. Those forgotten years long before his spell in Adelaide were drawing him; perhaps something important about himself was hiding there. Pansy could be helpful.

They were silent for a while. He sat on the sand to stretch his thighs and hamstrings the way Zoerner had taught him. One leg straight out, the other tucked up at the side. She watched and then copied.

'That's a good way to do it,' she said. Then she sat up, hugged her knees to her chin, and peered at him. 'You resented the fact I could keep up with you across that paddock. I know I was younger, but I was also just as tall as you. I think the main reason you resented it was that I was a girl. Am I right?'

He shrugged. 'I just don't remember all that.'

'You never wanted anything to do with Amy either, as I recall. When other kids teased her because she didn't want to talk or play with them, you just left her to endure it.'

He squirmed inwardly while showing her a smile. He knew she saw through it.

'I'm sorry. I don't want to judge the rights and wrongs of your past, Ted. It's just that you're going back to Adelaide and ... well, I'm very concerned for Amy. And for your mother.'

'Why?'

'I can't explain it all.' She frowned in thought. 'Would you say your father has been, ah, unpleasant at home lately?'

'Unpleasant?'

'Angry, nasty, threatening?'

He said nothing. He felt torn between guarding his privacy and unlocking things that strained for release. He turned away from her to gaze seawards. The pelicans still floated there, on the smooth gleam of the ocean, disturbed by neither doubts nor questions. No ripple from the past, no gust into the future shook their serenity.

Pansy waited without a word, and at last he faced her again. 'Yeah. It was what finally made up my mind about going back to Adelaide. I can't stand being around him anymore.' He felt a tightness in his throat pitch his voice unnaturally high.

Her tone softened. 'I've seen him giving Amy horrible looks. It was as though he hated her.'

'He was always pretty… um, *hard* on Mum and Amy.' Hard? Bloody cruel, now he thought about it. There were times when the man had shaken his wife so savagely his fingers left bruises on her arms. She might merely attempt casual conversation around the kitchen table and he'd fly into a rage. And Amy, even as a toddler, would avoid speaking to him. When her learning problems at school—which were, in fact, about avoiding the set work and drawing and writing poems and stuff instead—were reported, he tried to force an explanation out of her. Her refusal to speak made him so furious he picked her up and threw her into her room. Long sleeves were used to hide her bruises at school.

'Did he treat you like that?'

'No.' Except maybe just one time. As a rule, his father had gone out of his way to encourage him to succeed in things—especially sport. *Be tough, manly.* Growing up had been a matter of trying to be what his father wanted him to be. So he had taken the attitude that females should do what they were told and make life easy for the men.

'So, Ted, you're going to leave them alone with him.' She spoke softly but wouldn't let up and he had no answer. It was all too deep and difficult now.

With a big sigh he stood up and brushed dry sand from his body. 'Look, I have to finish my training.'

'Mind if I keep running with you?'

'Nope, but let's just concentrate on running, not chatter, eh?'

They kept at it for a good while. Although she wasn't beside him all the way, she never stopped until he did. He smiled again at the strangeness of it.

What would Oskar Zoerner say if he were here watching? But then, Oskar wasn't one to jeer at anyone for being different; a woman training like a footballer might not be beyond the pale for him. Other blokes— his workmates, for example—wouldn't accept it. And his father? Ted could almost hear him spitting every word of sarcasm he knew to shame his son for even being in the company of the *man-girl freak*.

After they had parted ways, he to the track back into town and she to some place where her normal clothes were, he could not stop thinking about his family. Amy — to become a famous artist, was she? She had always loved to draw, and later to paint, but he had never really looked at her pictures. Some people— women—would describe them as 'pretty' and 'beautiful', talk about how clever she was and so forth, but that was what females did, wasn't it?

He heard a harsh voice boom down at him. 'Drop that and get out of here! And don't let me ever see you do that again!' He was, instantly, inside his head, in the room where his sister painted. In his panic he dropped the brush and palette. They splattered onto the floor and a huge hand wrenched him by the ear out through the doorway.

'That's stuff for *girls*!' His father's voice was a half-whispered sneer. 'You're a *boy*! Remember what's between your bloody legs!'

Ted felt his eyes squeezed shut. His shoulders were suspended in a frozen shrug as he tried to pull

137

his head into them. Like a tortoise trying to protect itself from a hail of rocks hurled by a mob of boys.

He pulled himself upright and in haste looked around. He was standing on the track among mallee trees. No one watching, of course, but they would have stared. He took a very deep breath, shook his head and resumed his walking. How many years had that memory been locked away? He felt very small now as he walked this hard ground. Small and shaken.

Chapter 16

More and more people laid claim to tables in the tearooms. Pansy bustled among them, ensuring orders were taken and customers settled. Mrs Harding had taken the day off and left her in charge. Jenny was supposedly on duty but nowhere to be seen in the room.

'Jenny?' Pansy peered into the kitchen. 'Where are you, Jenny? I need help out here!'

She put her head out of the kitchen doorway into the storeroom just in time to see Jenny face her with a smile, while behind her a man disappeared through the back exit of the building.

'Yes, I'm coming.'

'You don't learn, do you, Jenny?'

The girl said nothing, but straightened her clothes and flitted past, maintaining the smile. Confident that Mrs Harding would not sack her; knowing, in the wake of recent events, that Pansy's influence over the owner would not extend that far. And smiling about it.

Pansy gritted her teeth and followed Jenny to attend to the tables. So that possum hunter was still hanging around; probably one of the gang causing trouble out on the farms. She recalled George Benson's complaint to the visiting government representatives. Could the poor man have been shot by a possum hunter?

The next two hours were busy. A little before closing time, with the people at the last tables apparently ready to rise, she heard very heavy boots enter the shop.

'Ah, Sergeant!'

'Good afternoon, Miss Pearce.'

'Come for a tea break, have you?'

'Afraid not. I wonder if we could talk for a few minutes?'

'Jenny, see to everything for a while, please.'

She led the policeman to a table on the veranda. His face wore the expression of granite, as usual.

'Miss Pearce, according to a number of people you are a friend of Mr Arthur Brewster-Leigh. You have been seen together at various times and locations. Would you explain your connection with him, please?'

'Arthur? Is he in trouble?'

'What is your connection?'

'I met him a few weeks ago. He came here to study wildlife with two other people from Adelaide, and I met them by accident. We had a few conversations.' She stopped and held his gaze. 'Enough?'

'Witnesses have told us you spend more than one or two passing moments with the man. What do you talk about, exactly?'

'Skinks ... yacca rats ... education ... preserving the bush ... '

'Yes. I gather he's very keen on all that—wants to stop farmers from clearing any land, in fact.'

'I'm not sure he wants to stop *all* clearing, but ...'

'So keen he's willing to be violent about it, wouldn't you agree?'

'No. He's ...'

'But, Miss Pearce, quite a number of witnesses say you intervened when he was fighting in the street. Do you deny that?'

'I beg your pardon? He was *not* fighting, Sergeant. He was being bashed around by a gang of drunken men ...'

'You were also present in the town hall when he had to be restrained from attacking Joe Benson. And Mr Brewster-Leigh on that occasion said Mr Benson should be *killed*. Do you recall that?'

The direction of the questioning was now clear and Pansy would stand for none of this. 'Arthur gets very excited about things he believes in, but he is *not* a violent man! He's actually a very gentle person, but because he has some unusual ways people simply don't understand him. He's an easy target for any bully who happens to be in the vicinity. It's been the story of his life, from school years onwards. Even his family ostracise him ...'

'Miss Pearce, for someone who has had just a few conversations with him, you seem to know him very well indeed.' He paused, studying her face, and, when she made no reply, cocked his head. 'You certainly have a habit of nosing your way into other people's business!'

She spied the barest hint of a sneer.

'You would agree, wouldn't you, that the man is *more* than *unusual*, as you described him?'

What was he talking about?

141

'Miss Pearce, I've received information from Adelaide about him. Your good friend is well known to police in the city. He's been at the centre of street disturbances. I believe Arthur Brewster-Leigh to be what learned scientists call a degenerate.' He was watching her face closely.

Who on earth was he talking about?

He continued. 'Small wonder he doesn't have many friends, eh?

What could she say to that? Bewildered, Pansy could only stare at the policeman.

He leaned towards her and shaped slow crisp syllables. 'But let's not dwell on that now. Apart from the town hall incident, did you *ever* hear him say anything about Joe Benson?'

Pansy also leaned forward to bring their faces very close. 'No.' She sat back in her chair again. 'But I can tell you who was really being aggressive towards Joe. The possum hunters. Joe said he had to drive them off his property. They were stealing. He said he was afraid it would come to a fight.'

The policeman frowned. 'Possum hunters? This is the first I've heard of anything like that. Can anyone else corroborate your story?'

Pansy explained how, Gerald being ill, she had acted as chauffeur to Mr Homburg and Mr Butler for the drive to the Benson homestead. She recounted the discussion between Joe and the parliamentarians.

'Miss Pearce, do you *really* expect me to question two of the most important men in the government about this murder?'

She shrugged. 'Just trying to help, Sergeant.' She watched him turn and walk away, shaking his head.

'So!' Pansy sighed, as she and Amy walked later that day through the coastal bush. 'It seems our fearsome Sergeant would rather follow his blind prejudice down the smoothest road to the nearest solution, rather than find the truth.'

'You never know. He might investigate the possum hunters after all, and pretend it was a track he discovered for himself. Men just don't like to admit that a woman's judgement could be better than their own.'

Pansy nodded. Her thoughts wound back to the conversation with Ted on the beach.

'How are you getting on with your brother now, Amy?'

'Funny you should ask that! Yesterday he behaved peculiarly. He walked in when I was painting and watched for a minute. Then he said he liked the work. Imagine that—Ted saying he *liked* something I did!' She stopped in her tracks and turned to Pansy. 'In fact, for him to even show an interest in what I do is rather remarkable. What made you ask about him?'

Pansy told how she and Ted had met on the beach and chatted about the past. 'He said he'd go back to Adelaide soon. I said that worried me.'

'Why?'

'Your father, Amy.' Seeing the query on her friend's face, she added, 'Come on now! You *know* he's been getting nastier than ever lately. I'm worried for you and your mum—and you'll have even less protection with Ted gone.'

They resumed their walk in thoughtful silence, picking their way to the crest of the steep slope above the beach. A startled skink scampered for cover under

143

a clump of grass. A hawk hung in the sky, searching the ground. Then suddenly, before their eyes, was a vista of wide blue ocean. Far out, the white sails of a ketch were bright in the late-day sunlight.

Pansy sat on an outcrop of rock. 'Now, I've been itching to ask you this. What did Lizzy tell you when I'd gone the other day?'

Amy sat beside her. 'What makes you think she told me *anything*?'

'Don't play games! I could tell she wanted to talk to you, but not while I was around. So I left to give her an opportunity.'

For a moment, Amy just stared across the ocean to the horizon. 'Yes, you were right. And it wasn't only Lizzy who talked. It was Mum too.' She closed her eyes. 'What they told me was … very new.'

'I'm all ears!'

Amy's gaze was again fixed on the far edge of the world as she slowly retold the old woman's story.

Lizzy's mother was the child of an English sailor and an aboriginal woman. The sailor settled on the island some years before the colony of South Australia was established, and made a living by hunting seals, kangaroos and wallabies for their skins. There were others like him. They would sail across Backstairs Passage and abduct aboriginal women, whose hunting skills and knowledge of the bush were invaluable to the men. Her father died when she was still a child.

'And so how is your mum related to Lizzy?'

'Lizzy's older sister was my mum's mother. Mum's father disappeared before she was born.'

'So Lizzy really is your aunty!'

Amy nodded slowly. 'Lizzy never married. Her sister and the baby—my mum—lived with her for quite a while. Lizzy and my mother were always together. Then Mum's mother married another man who took her to live close to Kingscote. It was a long way from Lizzy's place, and she knew her brother-in-law disapproved of her visiting. So she hardly ever did.'

Amy lapsed into silence and Pansy mused over the story as they both sat gazing across the ocean. So there was, after all, some substance to the notion that her friend was descended from aborigines, as children in her schooldays had insinuated in whispers and winks.

Pansy's thoughts returned to Lizzy. There was something else that still begged an explanation: why, during her visit to Mary and Amy, did the old woman seem so frightened that Jack might be in the house?

Amy replied to that question with a shrug. 'She *was* nervous, wasn't she? I think Mum understands. But neither of them said anything about it.' She folded her arms and hunched her shoulders as though she felt cold. 'I s'pose she feels the same as me about *him*!' Her shudder was visible.

Pansy felt that urgent pang: she had to find out more about Jack Dodd. It was not just her inborn curiosity that drove her; she was more and more convinced he was very dangerous to Amy and her family, and even to other people. She was sure he had a grizzly past that should be revealed, and perhaps only Lizzy could do that. The old woman seemed to harbour so much important information!

Amy rose and stretched. 'Anyway, I think I might see her again soon.'

'Do you mean Lizzy's visiting again?'

145

'Nope. I don't think she would take another risk of running into Dad. No, I'm going to paint a yacca out near Lizzy's hut.'

'Why? Aren't there plenty around here?'

'There's a special one. It has three crowns, or heads or whatever you want to call them. And it's very tall—more than ten feet—which means it must be very old. I saw it when I went to find Lizzy.'

Pansy chortled. 'You won't stop painting yaccas, will you?'

'There's something about them … Margaret Crump was right, you know. I *am* on the track of something I can only discover by painting them.'

A twang of memory shot yet another question to Pansy's tongue. 'So what was Lizzy trying *not* to say just before I left the three of you? She was talking about your yacca paintings too! Something about you having *the knowing* …'

Suddenly she found Amy's eyes looking into hers. Such a rare thing! The honey of those eyes was usually made difficult to savour, yet now … their direct boldness was arresting. Pansy held her breath, anticipating something she could not name.

'Pansy, she didn't want to say anything while you were there because she thought Mum and I wouldn't want anyone else to know. She was right—but you're the exception. Promise me that everything I'm telling you today will be kept secret.'

'Certainly! I won't talk about it to anyone outside your family …'

'No—not my father either! And Ted … maybe not even him. Oh, I don't know. I'll have to think about Ted.'

'I promise. Only you and your mother.'

Amy turned away again and pointed along the coastline. 'That's west, more or less. Right?'

'Right. Keep going along the coast and you'll come to the end of the island.'

Amy turned back and pointed past Pansy in almost the opposite direction. 'And across the sea that way is the mainland. Right?'

'Well, yes!' Pansy was impatient. 'We both know that, don't we?'

'What you don't know — and nor did I until Lizzy explained — is that we're in a special place.' Amy pointed again towards the mainland. 'Over there is where my aboriginal people came from. They understood their place in the world, and where they came from before that, and where they went to after that.'

Pansy listened to what she unfolded. The aboriginal people of the nearest mainland region — around Normanville and Yankalilla and Victor Harbour — believed that when they died their spirits would cross the waters of Backstairs Passage to the island and travel overland to its western end. There they would dive into the ocean and journey to the horizon. They would eventually enter the Sky World and eventually produce spirit children destined to be born on earth.

'The spirit children leave the sky and come back from the west through the sea and gather around the yacca trees. They have to wait there until it's time for them to go into the bellies of their mothers. And then …' Amy shrugged. 'Then nine months later they're born.'

Pansy said nothing. She scanned the broad vista from east to west and back again, allowing time for the

147

story to settle in. Mythology was not a subject she had investigated deeply. The stories of the Bible were, of course, very familiar to her. Couldn't avoid them, what with the Sunday readings her father made compulsory for the family; and their attendance at church whenever a minister was in Kingscote. The narratives of the Good Book were an integral part of her knowledge. Now, in a more sceptical adulthood, she was asking herself many radical questions about them, questions she had voiced to no one. So, if the Bible's framing of life, death and creation was questionable, how was she to treat this new tale from Amy's mouth?

'Amy, this is what Lizzy told you. But what has it to do with *the knowing*?'

'My paintings told her I somehow knew all this. It was in my blood, I suppose she meant, and it was finding its way into my pictures. The way I do the yaccas ... Remember what Mrs Crump said about the light I put around them and so on?'

'Do they mean, ah, you're showing the souls of the unborn hovering around the yacca?'

'Mmm, without really trying to do it. And I can't explain it—but I feel they're right in some way.'

Could there be any truth to this? It all made Pansy deeply uncomfortable. She held her tongue though, because it was clear her friend valued what Lizzy and Margaret had told her. As they walked home in wordless contemplation, she knew that to protect Amy she must continue to probe mysteries about the Dodds. But she could not do it Amy's way; it must be her own.

Chapter 17

Kenneth Maine placed a calming hand on Arthur's shoulder. 'Now take a moment for some slow deep breaths, old boy. No, don't talk. Breathe.'

Arthur did as he was told. Watching, Pansy saw Kenneth and Margaret were able to communicate with this man in a way nobody else apparently could. His earlier distraught gabbling had seemed unstoppable, yet here he was, sitting still and quiet now, his distress under control. And all because of the reassurance of Kenneth's quiet voice and touch.

Pansy's request that they meet away from town to talk over the police suspicion of Arthur had won instant agreement from Kenneth and Margaret. They were back on the island for another few days of work, and had cajoled their younger friend into coming along to the pond where Pansy was waiting.

As she outlined her conversation with Sergeant Lawrence the jerky movements of Arthur's limbs grew more and more frequent. The tipping point came with her recount of the policeman's allegation that Arthur had attempted to abduct children in Adelaide. The twitching body suddenly flew into a tirade of pacing, stamping and yelling. The man whose intellectual rigour and prodigious grasp of facts had earned him the highest respect of many learned people, whose appreciation and understanding of Australian species made him a champion of a national conservation campaign—that man vanished in an instant before Pansy's eyes. In an outraged tantrum, Arthur screeched his innocence like a young child.

Margaret grasped one of his hands in both of hers and almost sang a lullaby with her soothing words. 'Now, now Arthur ... you're safe with us ... let's make a cool examination of this situation.'

Kenneth placed himself firmly in front of Arthur and looked into his face. 'We will make your innocence clear. A scientific approach is the way, my boy.'

Now, with Arthur seated and silent, Pansy stared. They were mother and father to him. Under Kenneth's hand he was again breathing deeply, slowly.

She felt she could ask a question without sending him into another frenzy. 'Can you help me understand what *really* happened, Arthur? With those children?'

'It was on the banks of the River Torrens in Adelaide. I was on my way home from the university when I found a lizard sunning itself on a rock, just off the track. I went closer to look. Two boys were playing nearby and they came to see what I was looking at. Very noisy, they were. I had to make them walk quietly so it wouldn't be scared away.'

He fell silent. The listeners waited. A group of honeyeaters in the correa bushes across the pond burst into a sudden loud chorus. Their chittering bounced across the water.

'And then?'

Arthur drew another deep breath before continuing. 'It was a frill necked lizard, an unusually big one – spectacular, in fact. The boys were fascinated. So I started to tell them all about the species: how it lived, why it had all those frills around its neck, and so on. But the lizard moved off into the bushes, so we followed it while I continued teaching them about it. They were very keen to learn more ...' Again he stopped.

'And the boys' mothers saw them going with you into the bushes?'

He nodded. 'They ran after us, screaming ... They were such idiot women! They ...'

Kenneth's gentle hand on his shoulder pulled him back from another bout of rage. He sat hunched, his face buried in his hands.

Kenneth sneaked a glance at Margaret, winked at Pansy, and uttered an exaggerated yawn. 'We-e-ell now, shall we all go about our business for a while? We can come together again for a parley about how we should handle this matter – tomorrow perhaps?'

Margaret chimed in. 'Yes, I definitely need to do some sketching of those orchids I saw over the hill the other day.' She patted Arthur's hunched shoulders. 'And I'm sure Arthur has more to do in his survey.' Into his now upturned face she smiled. 'Right?'

He nodded and rose with a far more composed purposeful demeanour.

Pansy slapped her hands to underline the decision. 'Tomorrow it is, everyone. This seems like a suitable meeting place. Let's say half past five? We should all have finished work then.'

She watched Arthur stride off. His eagerness was very understandable. He found relief in the chance to throw himself into work rather than wrestle with the intense emotions triggered by his dealings with people.

Margaret went in another direction, her kit on her back. Before Kenneth could leave, however, Pansy detained him with a hand on his arm. 'The sergeant called him a *degenerate*. I've seen the word used a few times in the newspaper, of course, but the meaning was never really clear. I can tell it's meant to be derogatory. Could you explain?'

The man's face shone with pleasure at the opportunity to gather his immense knowledge into an *ex tempore* lecture.

'With pleasure, Pansy! It started with a fellow named Galton—in the 1880s, as I recall. A very influential chap he was. Started a lot of scientific activity that is still extremely influential today.'

She marvelled at the information this learned man reeled out, garnished with his own observations here and there. She could imagine how students in his university lectures would be stimulated to learn more. And he was a specialist in *geography*, which surely wouldn't cover matters like degeneracy.

He went on to say how Galton initiated the eugenics movement. He aimed to raise the quality of the human species to the optimum, by encouraging the ablest and healthiest people to produce more children. Galton's approach, later dubbed *positive* eugenics, differed from the push by *negative* eugenicists to cull those they deemed innately unfit from the breeding stock.

'Yes!' Kenneth saw her face screw up in distaste at the notion of humans as livestock. 'Yes, such scientists—and they are still with us, and thriving with many followers—want to treat the civilised world as a gigantic farm. The obvious question is: Who shall be the farmers?'

He continued with vigour. Names tumbled out in the academic's flowing account, names like Lombroso, Mendel, Davenport, Virchow … Would he ever stop?

Pansy struggled to retain the main points as they accumulated. 'So as it stands,' she leapt in when he paused for a breath, 'the medical scientists want to prevent the breeding of criminals and the immoral and slow learners and epileptics and the insane and paupers and vagrants … and goodness knows who else. The degenerates. Correct?'

'Well, not all doctors agree, but a significant number do think that way. They see certain types of individuals as defective—socially unfit—and liable to pass on their degeneracy by producing far more children than the rest of the population. And many people in other positions of authority have taken that view—even judges and educators.'

'And policemen, I've found.'

'Indeed. But not all, mind you. And I am friendly with one or two well-regarded lawyers who strongly oppose eugenics.'

When Pansy reached home after work the following day, her father was sweeping the veranda of the shop. An excuse for meeting her, she knew. He never swept the veranda in the afternoons—unless he wanted to see her coming home.

'G'day Dad.'

'Ah, Pamela. So you're finished for the day?'

She almost answered with sarcasm, but bit her tongue. 'Yes, Dad.'

He stood erect, broom held at his side. She was reminded of the military cadets she had seen on parade in Kingscote.

'I'd like a word, Pamela.'

'Certainly. There are several available. Which one?' Her inner censor was simply too slow to stop that one.

He closed his eyes with a barely perceptible sigh. 'Pamela, please! I want you to stop … stop getting involved in affairs that are none of your business. It's been one thing after another for the last few weeks and you're just getting yourself into trouble.'

'Trouble? I wasn't aware …'

'Pamela, the police are investigating you!'

She blinked. 'Investigating *me*? Not quite the right way to put it, Dad. Sergeant Lawrence asked me for information about … someone else. I told him all I could.'

His knuckles whitened on the broomstick. 'Well, it apparently wasn't good enough. Now it's not only the sergeant. Just a while ago there were two detectives from Adelaide asking about you—here in *my shop*!'

Detectives? The sergeant's superiors must have decided he wasn't up to the job. 'All's well, Dad. I'll go and find them.' She stepped off the veranda. 'And I'll tell them to put the questions to me in person from now on—and no more coming into *your shop*.'

His voice turned shrill behind her back. 'What? Pamela, you can't talk the police like that!'

She sniggered to herself out on the street.

The station was, as a rule, open two days a week, when a constable rode out from Kingscote. The sergeant would visit from time to time when he thought it necessary. Since the Benson murder, however, the building was inhabited daily, and this afternoon it seemed to be a hive of activity.

The constable faced her from behind the counter as she entered. Behind him the sergeant was at his desk with another man in plain clothes.

'Good afternoon, Miss Pearce. What can I do for you?'

'Good afternoon. I'm told you were asking for me.'

It was the sergeant's voice that responded from the background. 'You were correctly informed, Miss Pearce. We need to ask some questions—again.' He moved with deliberate nonchalance to the front of the room, eased the constable aside, folded his arms and set his eyes upon her. 'Questions concerning Mr Arthur Brewster-Leigh—again.'

He was about to say more when a quiet voice interrupted. 'Questions which *I* will ask this time.'

Never before had she seen the sergeant's steely gaze broken. His eyes narrowed and darted; his jaw muscles flexed. No love lost between these two then. But who was this man who could subordinate the sergeant? It was not the one who shared his desk, but another, emerging from the gloomy corner behind it. Another plainclothes man. Short in stature, he now stood beside tall and thin Lawrence.

'You can leave this to me, thank you sergeant.'

His uniformed colleague half clenched his fists as his arms unfolded. He stepped away very slowly, boot heels thumping the floor.

The short man extended his hand towards the corner he had come from. 'Miss Pearce, please have a seat at my desk. This way ...' He wasted no time getting to the point. 'I have come from headquarters in Adelaide to investigate the death of Mr Joseph Benson. I'm Detective Inspector Rod Neale.'

This man's voice was quiet but intense. His tone was so even it sounded unnatural. Pansy sensed some sort of contained malice searching for a target.

'Miss Pearce, how well did you know Joe Benson?'

'He was a customer at my father's store for as long as I can remember. He and his wife knew my parents quite well and I met them at social events occasionally. That was when I was younger, of course. Once I started working at my own job I had little contact with them.'

'You did meet them again not long ago, did you not?'

'Yes.'

'Yes, I know about that occasion, Miss Pearce.' The hint of a leer flickered around his mouth. 'Made quite a little jaunt of it, didn't you?'

'Jaunt? I don't ...'

'Do you have a license to drive a motorcar?'

'Yes, I ...'

'What instruction have you received in driving a motorcar?'

'I was taught by a government chauffeur — Gerald.'

'Gerald who?'

'I don't know his surname.'

'I see.' The detective sat back in his chair and spoke with slow precision. 'I would have thought that a *lady*, in seeking *driving* instruction, would be careful to first know the full identity of her chosen instructor.'

His raised eyebrows and interrogative silence were bait she could resist with contempt. She held his gaze and waited.

Now he let words dangle before her face like a banner. 'How many other *ladies* on Kangaroo Island drive cars, Miss Pearce?'

'I'm eager to know, Inspector. Do tell!' She saw a glare vanish from his face almost as soon as it had appeared.

He sat forward again, clasped his hands on the desk and spoke rapidly. 'Can you tell me anything that might help to find the murderer?'

'I can only say what I've already told Sergeant Lawrence. Joe Benson said there were possum hunters trespassing and stealing from his property. He had to chase them off, but at least one of them was quite aggressive. I think you'll find other farmers had trouble with them too ...'

'Ah, yes.' He flicked pages of a notebook and read from it. 'You claim that witnesses to Benson's statement were Mr Homburg and Mr Verran—both high ranking members of the State Government.'

'We were all sitting there at the same meeting, Inspector. Have you questioned *them*?'

'That's not for you to worry about, Miss Pearce!'

She could almost see the words as he extruded them through his teeth now. Was it time to ease off?

'I'm much more interested in a certain person widely known to have been aggressive with people here—and especially with Benson. He even said Benson should die.'

'Ah now, Inspector, we have come to your preferred candidate: the *degenerate*. Correct?'

The Inspector kept his hands firmly clasped on the desktop but raised an eyebrow. 'Are we referring to the same man, Miss Pearce?' When she made no effort to respond, he continued. 'The person I have in mind is one Arthur Brewster-Leigh. A person with whom, I am reliably informed, you are closely acquainted. Is that so?'

'I know Arthur.'

'And you were present when he had to be restrained from attacking Joe Benson.'

'He was yelling and angry. People did hold him but I'm sure he wouldn't have actually touched Joe.'

'Did you hear him threaten Benson with death?'

'He did not. He said something to the effect that people *like* Joe, who cut down yacca trees, should have no place on earth. You see, Arthur gets extremely upset about the loss of flora and fauna. He dedicates his life to educating people about Australian species and …'

'Miss Pearce, at least a dozen people who attended that meeting have stated they heard him scream a death threat at Benson.'

'Well … I know that's not what he meant. He's not the violent type!'

'What type is he then?'

Pansy paused. There was an arrogant derision in his tone. Was it directed at her — or at Arthur? Or both? 'Inspector, I bow to your greater knowledge. What type is he?'

'I have interviewed Mr Brewster-Leigh at some length. The man has abnormal movements in his arms and legs, even when sitting. In fact, I must say it was difficult to make him stay in a seat. I had to have Sergeant Lawrence stand behind him to stop him jumping around.'

Poor Arthur. This detective's interrogation would surely have upset him very quickly. Of course he would have been unable to control his movements.

'For a man of thirty years, his physique is obviously underdeveloped. His voice is also abnormal. And he lost his temper so easily and flew into the most incoherent raving.' The Inspector sat back and gazed through narrowed eyes at Pansy. 'Miss Pearce, your friend is not a normal individual.'

She could not hold back any more. 'He is an extremely intelligent man, highly respected in university circles! You need to be patient enough to listen to him explaining his philosophy, his aims for this island to become an immense schoolroom where people can learn to appreciate nature ...'

'That does not mean he is normal. I believe he is a danger to society, Miss Pearce. You see, I have come across him before – in Adelaide. I had to interview him concerning complaints that he tried to lead young boys into ... Well, I won't go into that.' The detective brought a firm hand down on the desk. 'He's a degenerate. I have dealt with a good number of degenerates in my time and I think I will have to add him to the list – for the sake of society.'

'So you're one of the negative eugenicists. What's your preference, Inspector: sterilisation or incarceration? Or do you skip both and head straight for execution?' The sharpness of her tone made his composure disintegrate for a moment. To maintain her dominance, she rose quickly, making the chair squeal loudly on the floorboards. 'Inspector, you won't find

Arthur the easy victim you assumed him to be. He's innocent, and I'll be marshalling strong defence on his behalf. I have influential contacts. Don't bother to see me out.'

Pansy gritted her teeth as she strode along the street. The police were intent on convicting Arthur. Kenneth Maine would have to call on his lawyer friends immediately.

The lemon in Mary Dodd's hand was large and still tinged with green in places. She had plucked it from the tree in the backyard. 'The first one this year.' She took a knife, sliced thin round pieces onto a plate, and placed it in the centre of the table.

The odour was clean and strong and tantalising in Pansy's nostrils. She picked one of the slices and let it slip into the steaming cup of tea on the table before her.

'I've been down to Lizzy's place three or four times.' Amy took a lemon slice too. 'There are some very interesting views around there. I did more sketches. But today I took my paints and easel. I think I've got another piece to put in the yacca series.'

'Good.' Pansy sipped her tea, relishing the lemon tang. 'How's Lizzy?'

'She doesn't talk a lot. Sits on her old chair outside the hut, with her dogs all around her. She seems to doze off a few times during the day.'

Mary stirred her tea. 'She's old. Needs to rest more.' She sighed, staring out through the kitchen window. 'But you should have seen her when I was little. She could darn near outrun a wallaby! And she'd dive off a boat and swim underwater until you'd think

160

she'd never come up again—and then bob up with shellfish for dinner!'

'Mum, she wants to come and see you again.'

'Good. I'd like to see her again too. Would you take the buggy out to get her?' Mary lowered her gaze. 'Just make sure it's when your father is well out of the way.'

Chapter 18

He left the stables, mentally ticking off another day from the calendar. March lay just a little way ahead — then Adelaide. But each day of work now felt longer to Ted than the last, longer and more tiring. Today the pub had little allure: listening to blokes try to outdo each other with their stories of all the hard yakka they had done to earn their schooners was just too wearisome. No, this was time to go home.

He passed the lodging house where employees of the Dodd brothers lived. Down one side of the building, half-hidden by a gum tree, was Jim, the saltie his father had taken on for a short term. Talking to someone else, holding out his hand as the other placed a pound note into it, then another and another.

He remembered that time in the pub, when his father had agreed to give Jim a job, lied about being short of men, and took him out of earshot to explain a condition of employment. Today Jim's job had finished. And now a glimpse of the other man's head told Ted the hand feeding him money belonged to his father.

Ted slowed his walk and watched. Their position and manner suggested they wanted to avoid attention. The notes gathered in Jim's palm amounted to considerably more than the wage due for the few days worked. And now what was this? The hands from behind the tree handed to Jim some large object—more than a yard long, wrapped in a lot of cloth. Jim listened for a few moments, nodded, shook hands and headed off towards the back entrance of the lodging house.

Ted turned away and quickened his pace before his father could see him.

His thoughts were still on the mysterious package next morning, when he stood at the stables, as usual, overseeing the men as they harnessed their horses and prepared drays for the day's carting. His father arrived, slapped a few backs and raised some laughter with his jokes. He stood beside his son. 'Plenty o' bags waitin' out there, Ted—on Harrison's block and Cowan's too. There'll be a few loads on the other blocks by tomorrow. Keep the boys moving, right?'

Ted watched him yawn and massage his eyes with both hands.

Another voice came from behind them both. 'Another night wasted on poker and grog?'

Jack did not turn at all. He exhaled in a loud hiss and rolled his eyes to the sky.

George patted Ted on the back. 'Plenty of work for the drays, lad. And there'll be a lot more soon. We've got contracts for six more properties, and that won't be the end either. The expansion is going ahead, young feller! I hope you're thinking about what we discussed?'

Ted saw a dark glance from his father, who then turned away instantly.

His uncle continued. 'Anyway, Ted, I need you to drive me to Kingscote. Grab the sulky, would you?'

The younger brother spun around. 'What? I've got him leading all the carting …'

'I'm sure you can see to that easily yourself for a few hours, Jack. I have to be in Kingscote to collect my new motorcar.' He put a hand on Ted's shoulder. 'The first of a fleet for this business, right m'boy?'

At this, the face of Ted's father flashed with pain. An instant later it flared with rage. He stormed away from them, fists clenched.

The sulky had travelled hardly a quarter of a mile when Uncle George told him to stop. 'I have to slip into the coppers' station to see Inspector Neale. He needs some information.' He winked. 'Won't be long.'

No more than ten minutes later they were on their way again. The older man chuckled. 'Nice feeling to know you've helped our defenders of justice to do their job!'

'Eh?'

'Oh, best not to divulge, Ted. I'll just leave the good inspector to pursue his investigations.'

There was a sly smugness in his uncle's tone Ted did not like. And *the good inspector* had a reputation in Adelaide: Oskar Zoerner had more than once mentioned the man as the ugly side of the police force, although he had not given any detail. What 'help' was Uncle George giving Neale?

They passed the general store, where James Pearce was sweeping his veranda. He waved and they reciprocated.

Uncle George relaxed into his seat. 'He'll be a beneficiary of our business expansion. We'll buy more of his hardware, tools and such like. And he might be a good ally to help stop that bloody push for making the island a reserve, eh?'

'Oh yeah, he might.'

'You reckon we could get him to shut his ratbag daughter up?'

Ted looked at him and shrugged. This conversation was going in an uncomfortable direction. Perhaps it was best not to encourage it.

'I mean stop her from helping the preservationists. Maine and his woman, and that other one …'. He snorted. 'The *degenerate*.'

Ted remained silent. He wasn't sure what he would say in any case—and his uncle seemed content to do all the talking for now.

'Have you heard, boy—the latest news about her? The Pearce girl? You boys call her *Pansy*, don't you? She's been seen running naked on the beach!' He guffawed into the tops of the gum trees along the roadside. 'What a sight that'd be, eh? Might answer the question everyone's asked for years. Is she actually a bloke?'

Ted winced at the slap on his shoulder. The man's laughter was hideous.

He walked into the house and found Amy in her studio, seated before a painting on an easel, brush in hand. And by the window was Pansy. The late light had almost left the room.

'G'day, ladies.'

165

Amy turned, eyes wide. 'Well, another one for the books! Have you ever come in here before?'

His answering thought did not pass his lips. *Yes, there was another time you don't know – nearly twenty years ago. I was hauled out by the ear.* He caught himself retracting his head, and turned it into a shrug.

He looked at Pansy, who was staring out of the window. 'You look a bit down in the dumps.'

Her head turned slowly. 'It's been a fair cow of a day.' She stood up straight. 'I was sacked.'

How could that be? Pansy, the woman who was to rise to the top of the business world? His jaw dropped as she continued.

'Mrs Harding heard too many stories about me. Such as how the police have been questioning me because they think I had something to do with Benson's murder. And apparently I've been seen by everyone cavorting stark naked on the beach. Not good for business, when customers keep muttering things like that about the woman in charge of the shop.'

'So what will you do? Work for your father again?'

She shook her head. 'That wouldn't last a day.' She pulled herself taller and flexed her shoulders. 'But, don't worry. I'll find my way.'

They all held their own thoughts. From outside the window came a wattle bird's call, like staccato scrapes of metal.

After some time, Ted nodded towards the painting. 'Nice yacca. Must be very old.' It was one of those with several crowns, all stemming from a single black trunk. He took the age of the very young boy at its foot to be about four years, and remembered being told the plant grew about half an inch a year. 'Could have been growing for two or three centuries, maybe more.'

Amy glanced at Pansy. 'So this one was big even when our people came across from the mainland.'

'Eighteen thirty-six?' Ted assumed she meant when South Australia was first colonised.

His sister shook her head quite assertively. 'No. They came years before that, Ted. *Our* people did anyway.'

'But ...' He paused when they again looked at each other and then at him with serious faces. 'Our people? Do you know something I don't?'

The story she reeled out next was new, of course, but it was obvious why it had not come to light before. Descent from aborigines, from 'darkies', was always hidden if possible. Someone had once told him a jumbled yarn about whites living on the island before the colonisers arrived — American and British sealers, escaped convicts and aborigines from Tasmania — but it was not part of the official history he remembered from school.

He listened in silence until Amy finished. 'This Lizzy ... how do you know she's got it right? She could be just stirring the possum!'

'Mum knows her well, Ted. As I said, they spent all their time together until Mum married Dad. Mum has no doubts Lizzy's telling the truth.'

Pansy spoke for the first time in a while. 'And Lizzy knows your father, Ted. She visited again today and told your mother a few things about him. Things you — we — should worry about.'

He listened as she continued.

Chapter 19

'They've arrested Arthur!'

Margaret Crump's call came from across the street. At the door where she was talking with Ted and Amy before going home, Pansy turned and saw the woman run towards her. She arrived gasping for breath.

'The police have taken Arthur into custody!'

'Without evidence? How can they do that?'

'Someone saw a rifle in his room, hidden behind the wardrobe, and reported it to the police. Arthur had no license for it. He's detained pending further inquiries.' Margaret groaned and shook her head. 'Poor Arthur has probably never even touched a gun in his life, Pansy.'

'I'm sure. It wouldn't matter to Inspector Neale. He made it clear to me he intended to take Arthur out of circulation somehow.'

'Neale's a rogue.' Ted's tone was grim. 'My boss in Adelaide says he's dead crook.'

Pansy stepped closer and looked intently at him. 'Ted, do you think he might be rogue enough to lie about this gun?'

He stared back at her. She watched his pupils dwindle, his mouth hang open. Was he seeing something horrible for the first time?

'Uncle George ...' He swallowed. 'This morning he went into the station to give some sort of information to Neale. To help him with his investigations, he said. But he wouldn't say exactly what it was about.' He eyed the three faces slowly. They waited.

Pansy watched him shake his head and turn away. He had a lot to take in: first what he had heard earlier from Amy, when she retold Lizzy's story; then the added suspicion that his uncle was conspiring with crooked police to convict an innocent person. There was weariness in his stance now, those broad shoulders slumped in a way she had never seen before.

Pansy returned to the Dodd house. Amy was packing her kit for a trip into the bush. 'I have to get that scene onto canvas,' she said. 'There's a yacca with three tops ... three crowns, or heads or whatever ... it means a lot, and it has to be just right.'

'Out near Lizzy's hut?'

Amy nodded.

The pair walked together to the stable. From the horse's back, Amy looked down at Pansy gravely. 'Margaret and Lizzy are right. I'm finding the truth by painting. Something happened near that yacca. I know it's the one now. And there was a little boy ...' Her voice trailed away.

'Not Benny?'

Amy shook her head.

Pansy waved and the horse trotted away. All firm ground was softening, shifting. What next? Now Lizzy's old voice rang in her mind.

Them Dodds, they were bad'uns. Their father sold skins – possum, wallaby. Lived by himself when I was little. My mum told me never to go near him 'cos he'd hurt me. One day we saw him ride away for a few days somewhere and then he came back with a woman – well, no more than a girl she was – and 'e kept her out there in the bush away from everyone. I lived with my mother not far from 'em, but he made sure we never got near enough to talk to her. He'd get his gun if anyone came close ... took a shot at us once when we walked past a hundred yards away.

They had children. Boys. They went out hunting and sometimes I'd hide in the scrub and watch them. They did horrible things to possums and lizards, just for fun, dip rags in kerosene and tie them to the animals' tails an' set fire to 'em. And they laughed their heads off.

One day them boys, they saw me working in our vegetable garden. They crept up behind an' grabbed me. They try to drag me into the bush. One put his hand over my mouth but I bit 'im an' he took his hand away an' I hollered. My mother came runnin' out with our dogs an' them boys cleared off.

That was George and Jack. Their mother had another boy. Poor littl'un. He was only there for about four or five years.

Lizzy's experience of Jack Dodd shed light on her apprehension during her visits. But the youngest brother; what had happened to him? When Pansy asked, Lizzy only shook her head and changed the subject.

'Sacked?' James Pearce dropped the bag of flour onto a pile, straightened and stared at his daughter. 'And what reason did she give?'

'Reason? Quite *un*reasonable, actually. All based on gossip, prejudice ...'

She saw his raised eyebrow. Was he hiding a smile?

'Look, I simply came to tell you so you'd understand why I'm not at work. I don't want to argue about it.'

'No argument, Pamela. Oh, damn flour all over me! How does so much get out of those bags?' He grabbed a cloth from a hook on the wall, wiped his hands and tried in vain to brush the white stuff off his apron. With a hiss of exasperation, he flung the cloth away. 'Pamela, listen ... I'm sorry it came to this. I really am. But your behaviour over the last few weeks has not helped —'

'What's that?' Pansy rushed to the front door and onto the store's veranda. She knew the sound. Her heart beat faster. 'Yes!'

The vehicle was the same as the one she had driven for the two government men — a Maxwell Tourer — but green. George Dodd's hands were on the steering wheel. He sported a driving jacket, cap and goggles. He brought the motorcar to a halt outside the pub.

Pansy was drawn away from the store and along the road towards the beautiful machine. Oh, to grip that wheel again and feel the power her foot could command!

Ted, seated on a dray, reined in his horses and they both stopped beside the car together. She returned his nod and their attention returned to the

Maxwell. The eyes of a dozen or so men from the pub did the same.

Among them was Jack. For a second, her stomach felt queasy at the sight of his face. The narrowed eyes blazed, the flared nostrils and twitching lips like a threatened dog about to snarl.

'Feast your eyes, gentlemen! You're looking at the entrance to the future.' George was standing on the running board of his car. He faced the gathering and patted the deep green bonnet as he spoke. 'The power. The speed. The promise of prosperity — with much less of the hard yakka!'

Pansy saw how he enjoyed luring and guiding them. One by one the men stepped off the veranda to have a closer look. They peered at the controls, walked around the vehicle with murmurs of admiration, while he looked down on them from the car, hands at his chest pinching the edges of his waistcoat.

George continued loudly. 'Have you ever seen twenty-five horses look so beautiful? That's right — this clever contraption ...' He paused and turned to face his brother who was now the only man on the veranda. 'This *contraption* has the power of twenty-five horses packed into its engine. Think of what it can do!'

Jack turned away, swallowed all the beer from his glass and stood for a time with his back to everyone. George, meanwhile, answered questions about the car from one admirer after another.

Ted handed the reins to his partner and climbed down from the dray to stand beside Pansy. 'What d'you think?'

'I'd love to be driving it!'

'He's planning to use lorries for carting ...'

'Ted!' His father's tall frame had suddenly appeared beside them. 'Is that load all at the wharf now?' His question was curt. 'Right. You'd better take the horses to the stables and—'

'Ted knows that!' George Dodd, hands on hips, stepped towards them. 'Doesn't need to be told. Do you Ted?' He looked his brother up and down and sneered. 'But *you* just took the afternoon off, to sit on your arse and drink?'

George lay a fond hand on his nephew's shoulder. 'Ted, listen. I have to go and pay off Jim over there. His last day, you know, and he'll be taking the ship back to Adelaide. Won't be long. Just stick around and keep your eye on my motorcar, would you, son?'

Ted's father spun on his heel and stalked away towards his house. Ted moved closer to the car and began to inspect it. His uncle joined a man waiting some distance from the crowd, shook his hand and handed him an envelope.

Pansy bit her lip as she thought of Mary, alone in the house, and her husband approaching in a savage state. He had hurt her in the past, as Ted and Amy had told her. Would he do it again?

After two minutes she could not stop herself. She walked to the door of the Dodd house and knocked, but did not wait before opening it cautiously. She stepped inside. The voices she heard set off a churn of unease in her stomach. She froze and listened. Jack's voice was like a hammer, Mary's like a gurgling brook in comparison, but he quickly grew more aggressive and she responded firmly. Mary squealed. And squealed again.

173

Pansy darted down the hall, glancing into one room after another. Where were they? Another squeal, from the studio.

Before she got there he snarled something. It sounded like 'Is she near three trees?'

When she burst in, Mary was on her knees. He had one of her wrists twisted behind her back and his other hand gripped her jaw. He leaned over her, face only inches from hers.

'Let her go!' Pansy stopped barely two paces from them.

His surprise showed for a second, to be replaced by a sneer. 'Whatta you doin' here? Get outa my house!' His grip on Mary did not loosen.

Pansy took the last two steps. Standing over him, she put her right leg behind both of his, hooked her right arm around his throat and heaved. He gave a choking gasp, let go of Mary and fell.

'Aargh!' His recovery from the tumble was quick. He stood up and moved towards the door. 'I'll be back for you, you weird bitch!' And then he was gone. Seconds later the front door banged open.

'Are you all right, Mary?'

'Yeah.'

'What was that about?'

Mary massaged her face. The deep red marks of his grip would turn black and blue before long.

'He saw me looking at Amy's painting—that *Yacca and Child*. He knows that place. Lizzy said he would. He picked it up and smashed it.'

The painting lay on the floor, frame broken and canvas ripped. Pansy stared aghast at the remnants of all Amy's careful work.

'He was raving like a madman. I told him it wouldn't make any difference to smash it now… it was too late to hide the truth. I said Lizzy told me …' She winced and nursed a wrist with the other hand. 'Oh! That hurts.'

Pansy helped her to a chair.

'Well, that did it. As soon as I said her name he wanted to know where Lizzy was. I managed to hold it back. But I think he worked it out from the picture.'

'The big yacca with three heads … Sounds as if he's after Lizzy. Maybe to stop her from talking anymore? He's dangerous in the state he's in, don't you think?'

The two women's eyes met.

'Amy!' Pansy exclaimed the name. If Amy was out there near Lizzy's place she too could be in danger from her father's violent frenzy. 'I'll get someone to stay with you for a while, Mary. To make sure you're all right. Just sit and rest for a while, all right?'

She rushed out of the house and up the road to her parents' place. It was only two minutes before her sisters were bustling to Mary's side and Pansy was trotting towards the mob outside the pub, where Ted barred curious men from climbing into the Maxwell Tourer.

'Your mother's hurt, but it doesn't look too serious and she's being looked after.'

'What—'

'Your father. He's gone mad as a meat axe, Ted!'

His eyes widened. 'He's on his horse. Rode out of town just a while ago—in a hurry.'

She slapped his shoulder. 'Come with me!'

Chapter 20

Ted searched wildly around the car seat for something to grip. 'Well at least keep this thing in one piece! He'll have my guts for garters if it's harmed!'

'Don't worry about your uncle—I know what I'm doing. It's your father we have to deal with. He's dangerous.' Pansy trained her vision on the road ahead in an effort to avoid the largest potholes. The wheel tugged and jerked her hands violently, but the car kept a more or less even course.

She recalled voices shouting when she and Ted had jumped into the Maxwell outside the pub.

'Hey, look out boys!'

'She's at it again!'

One of them she knew to be George Dodd's. 'Stop her! Grab her, you useless bastards!'

No doubt her father would by now know his daughter was a car thief. He probably wouldn't be surprised. And Mrs Harding would be glad she could tell customers she had already sacked the Pearce girl. Still, that wouldn't matter anymore. The *Pearce girl* was on a new path into the future.

She slowed the Maxwell as it approached a sharp bend. Not far ahead would be a narrow track which they would have to cover on foot to reach Lizzy's hut.

As she left the bend behind and accelerated, she glanced at Ted. He had been grim and silent for quite a while. 'When do you go back to Adelaide?'

'A few days.'

'S'pose you'll be glad to go.'

'I'm just thinking about Amy right now. D'you really know where you're going?'

'Yep. Right … here!' Pansy slowed and halted. 'We have to leave the car here. C'mon!' She led at a trot along the track through scrub towards the coast. 'He couldn't have been here long before us.' A minute or two later she stopped and looked around. 'There!' The little-used path was easy to miss, but she knew it was there. 'That takes us to where Amy should be.'

They moved more slowly, pushing branches out of their way, and soon were in a clearing. On the other side stood the great yacca, its three big bristling heads catching sparks of late sunlight from the blue sky. A saddled horse was grazing. And, in the middle of the clearing, sat Amy.

Startled by the sudden appearance of other people, she dropped her drawing and stood up. 'What—?'

Pansy embraced her. 'Thank God you're safe!'

Amy waited but the arms clung on. Eventually she prised them loose and stepped back to scrutinise the two faces.

Ted spoke first. 'Have you seen Dad?'

'No.'

'We think he came here looking for Lizzy.'

177

Amy turned her palms skyward, shrugged, and shook her head.

'He's in a violent mood, Amy! He hurt Mum and —'

The three heads turned. The distant yell came from far beyond the clearing. 'Get up!' A man's brutal voice.

'Come on!' Pansy was sure she detected the direction. 'He must have got Lizzy!' She charged past the immense yacca and into the scrub, following an overgrown track.

A gunshot cracked. It came from straight ahead. She kept running, aware the other two were just behind her.

Another shot — this time much closer.

Also much closer was the man's voice as he yelled once more. 'Don't try to run again!' It was Jack. An old woman's weak groans followed.

The track stopped where the scrub stopped; at another clearing where Lizzy's hut stood. Her old chair was on its side. A dead dog lay nearby, blood marking where the bullets had entered.

So where had Jack taken Lizzy?

'This track goes to the cliffs.' Amy ran and the others followed.

A little way along the track lay another dead dog. Both must have died protecting the old woman.

The scrub gradually gave way to lower scattered bushes. They paused. Pansy made a quick reckoning of the location. They were at most fifty yards from the brink of a gorge, which conducted a river into the nearby sea. She had been here before, on hikes some years ago. Those cliffs were a near vertical drop, treacherously high in some places.

178

'There!' Ted whispered one chill word.

They looked where he pointed. Through gaps in the bushes two figures were visible, less than fifty yards away. Facing them was Lizzy, the brink of the cliff not far behind her. Jack Dodd, holding a pistol at his side, had his back to them.

Pansy lay a restraining hand on Amy's shoulder. 'Voices down. Heads down too! He's in a shooting mood, so best not let him know we're here yet.'

They stooped and followed her through the scrub. After a minute she signalled to stop. Crouched together behind bushes, they could make out Lizzy's croaked words.

'Same place you took your little brother, eh? Can't stop killin' now, can you, boy? That Benson feller first ... now me!'

'Keep movin' back ...'

Pansy heard movements somewhere back in the scrub behind her. She turned but saw nobody. But she was sure she heard feet crunching in twigs and leaf litter.

'No!' Lizzy's voice was suddenly stronger than ever. 'Stay away, girl!'

Amy rushed out of hiding towards her father. 'Leave her!'

He spun around with pistol raised, and fired.

Amy froze. At the same moment, Lizzy rushed at his back with a yell, arms reaching. But he twisted around and grabbed her with one arm under her chin, holding her by the throat against his chest. The other hand kept the pistol aimed at Amy. His face contorted with fury. 'You little bitch! You couldn't keep your snoopy nose out—'

Pansy strode out of cover. She heard Ted follow suit. Keeping her eyes on Amy, a few paces ahead, she signalled him to stop. They were spaced wide enough to make it hard for the gunman to cover all at once. 'Amy, don't go any closer!'

Jack took two steps back. 'Oh that'd be right—the man-girl freak too! And ... you, boy?' His mouth hung open for a second or two as he spotted Ted. His raised arm sagged and the gun pointed earthwards. 'Thought there was hope for you, boy. Turnin' against your old man, are you?'

Ted took another step forward. 'Put the gun down. *Please* Dad!'

Jack jerked the gun up and stepped backwards again, dragging Lizzy with him. 'Don't come any closer—any of you! Or I'll finish you as easily as I got rid of Benson—' He broke off and stared somewhere to his left.

Pansy twisted her head in time to see Sergeant Lawrence grunt and gasp his way from the bushes to be the fourth person confronting Jack Dodd in the open.

It was the moment Lizzy chose to screech like a cockatoo.

Pansy heard a cry leap from her own throat. She saw the old woman heave herself backwards, making Jack lose his balance.

Jack Dodd staggered back two steps. There were sudden gasps and a scream when they both disappeared over the edge of the cliff.

Chapter 21

A cool salty breeze seemed to pervade Pansy's body from head to toe; cleansing, invigorating, assuring. In Amy's eyes she saw uncertainty and excitement alternately flicker. But her own eagerness for the future was unadulterated. Leaning on the ship's rail, she knew this was meant to be; it was all clear now. Why had understanding taken so long?

'Hey, look!'

Amy's arm reached out over the ship's wake to show a pod of dolphins in pursuit. How many? Impossible to tell, as one or two would break the surface here while others disappeared again there.

'So fast!'

'They're catching us!'

The dolphins were soon gambolling alongside the vessel, chuffing from their blowholes and keeping pace with ease. Amy and several other passengers joked and commented to each other as they watched. Overhead, silver gulls swooped and circled. Pansy laughed into the gentle wind. The natural world seemed to be celebrating their departure from the island, their venture into a life still to be created.

She had announced the momentous decision some weeks back, to her family seated in their living room, Amy standing beside her. The quivering uncertainty in her abdomen threatened to erupt into her voice, but she kept her speech under control. Before she had even half finished, her sisters wept a little and her mother a little more. Her father remained impassive until all had been said.

Then he locked his gaze with hers. For seconds they did not move. When his face crinkled into a small wan smile Pansy felt tears well in her eyes for the first time since early childhood. And she could not remember any embrace like that which followed. The strength and tenderness of his hands on her back came as a shock. Her tears flowed freely.

How did Amy feel, standing amid this familial love? She had lived all her life in a household squashed and silenced by an omnipresent threat; her own father. He was a tormented soul unable to love, an agent of violent forces that erupted from somewhere deep in the past. He was now dead. Her own origins were still vague and, with Lizzy dead, probably destined to remain so.

'Well, I have a good brother,' she said when Pansy showed concern for her, 'and he's getting even nicer. He promised to see me often in Adelaide. We'll both visit Mum often and send her money from the city, and she'll inherit quite a bit of property anyway. Not that it makes up for losing Lizzy. She'll take a while to stop grieving over that.'

The dolphins veered away eventually and the passengers dispersed. One of them—stocky, face adorned with a thick drooping moustache—remained by himself, surveying the waters of Backstairs Passage and the coast of the mainland that now swelled on the horizon ahead.

Pansy recognised the German horseshoe buyer who had knocked on the front door a few months ago. So he must have made another trip to the island, and in the ship's cargo would be another load of old iron to be sold on to the agents in Port Adelaide, and taken to the munitions factories in Germany. As would the yacca gum; that, too, was on board. So many people worked so hard to harvest all those grasstrees, while also locked in a furious battle with just as many others wanting the harvest to cease. The struggle had even led to murder.

She turned to Amy. 'Did Margaret Crump say she'd meet us when we dock?'

Amy nodded. 'She collected the paintings I sent and had them taken to the house.'

Pansy tried to picture the house, bequeathed by her grandparents to her mother. It was years since she'd last seen it, but it would be their home now. The child-eye view in her memory projected the image of huge rooms with high, ornate ceilings. Perfect for hanging paintings.

'Work to do!' Amy smiled wide. 'I'll need to get the yacca series into shape for an exhibition she's planning.'

'Will you tell people what the aborigines said about the yacca? If you describe how the spirits of the unborn hover around the plant while waiting to enter a mother's body, you might add some spice to the paintings. That could help to sell ...'

'No.'

183

'Why?'

'If I tell them they won't really understand. I'll let them find it, maybe just feel it for themselves through my painting. If they can know it in their own way, it will mean more to them.'

They mused for a moment, wind playing around faces and tugging at their hats.

'Besides,' said Amy, pressing her fingertips to her moist eyes, 'if I tell people they're sure to ask how I know about it. I don't want to discuss that.'

Pansy had to agree. What would either of them ever want to say to strangers about the past few months? Too much hatred and fear, sadness and loss.

Amy shook her head slowly as she looked across the sea. 'I love art, but I have no idea how much money I can make from it. I might have to find other work.' Her face brightened. 'But where there's life, there's hope! Pansy, have you thought any more about how you'll earn a living in Adelaide?'

'Ah. At first it might be just some sort of waitress job. You know, something I can do easily to bring in some money quickly.' She chuckled into the wind then as she remembered the expression on Mrs Harding's face just a few days ago.

Her former boss had bustled up with feigned magnanimity and offered to give back the job at the tearooms. 'A second chance, my girl. I've thought it over, and I believe you could reform.'

The word had got around that advertisements for the vacant position had brought no one capable of filling it. Pansy managed some solemnity in her reply. 'I will indeed reform, Mrs Harding. And I will start in Adelaide.'

She stopped laughing and returned her gaze to Amy. 'Yes, I'll just do what I know for a while. But in the long run? I want to help people, Amy. I'll find a job that lets me help the people everyone else casts aside or treads on or persecutes ...' She chuckled. 'There are one or two I can think of already!'

'Who?'

'Connie Pincombe. Little Benny. And yes, even Arthur!'

Sergeant Lawrence had released Arthur immediately after the terrible event on the clifftop. He had ridden after Pansy and Ted when George burst into his office to complain of the theft of his car. From where he stood in the scrub near the cliff's edge he saw and heard enough to know that Jack Dodd intended to kill Lizzy and Amy and anyone else he saw as a threat, just as he had killed Benson. An inquest held in the Ocean View Hotel later heard from everyone involved in the clifftop incident, and the coroner decreed there was no criminal case to be made.

Jack would clearly be declared guilty of Benson's murder; his incriminating utterances just before death could be stated in court by four witnesses. An examination of the rifle from Arthur's room revealed no evidence that would definitely connect it with the murder. Ted was sure his father and uncle paid the salt worker to climb through the open window of the boarding house and slip it behind the wardrobe. So Arthur was now free and back in Adelaide. He would probably be called to give evidence in court, but there was no suggestion he was guilty of any crime, although one policeman would still be keen to pursue him.

'Inspector Neale—now there's someone I'm not anxious to meet again, Amy! But … for some reason, I suspect I will have to deal with him one day.'

'And I don't want to have anything to do with my Uncle George.'

Pansy nodded. George. Ted had suspected his uncle of underhanded malicious deeds. But in the end police found no evidence of wrongdoing on his part. In ostentatious big-heartedness he announced to all he would not lay a charge of car theft on Pansy and Ted, and his business affairs would no doubt proceed without interruption.

She stretched her arms overhead and drew a deep breath of briny air. Kangaroo Island was no longer visible astern. They were past Cape Jervis and well into the Gulf of St Vincent now; the scattered rooftops of Normanville steadily slipped behind them as *Karatta* steamed northward. Mottled blue-greys and browns on the long coastline ahead were interspersed with green, brought on by the late autumn rains. About three hours would bring them to the Port Adelaide wharf.

'I think, Amy, when we're much older we'll remember nineteen thirteen as the year our lives began again.' She giggled. 'We can tell Inspector Neale we're *re*generates!'

As they laughed together, she let her hand cover Amy's. Their fingers entwined. With the enfolding of warm skin, she knew she was, at long last, where she belonged. In her mind, a single word sang louder than all the noise of wind and ship and sea. *Forever.*

Three giant heads looked down on the little boy, who was building a small house with twigs. A woman watched him add one at a time. A breeze from the wide azure sky shook coruscations of sunlight from the thick bristles on the heads. They sat on black necks all branching from a single tall black trunk.

The little boy giggled as he proceeded with his building. 'Three-tree's laughing, mummy.'

She glanced up at the heads of the huge yacca towering over her and her son. To him it was always a sort of person, one who spoke to him. 'Why's he laughing, littl'un?'

''Cos all the fairies are playing tricks. Listen.' He chortled again.

He often played this game with some kind of spirit-beings he believed hung around the yacca. 'Fairies? Where are they?' Playing along with him, she turned and looked at the ground behind.

'Not there, silly!' He pointed up towards the looming heads. 'Up there. All in the air around him.'

'Oh! What are they saying?'

He gave no answer, but continued building with an occasional giggle.

Author's Notes and Further Reading

**History of Kangaroo Island—
aborigines, extinguished species, settlers**
For a fascinating and well-documented account of Kangaroo Island history, particularly concerning the aborigines brought to live there, I recommend *Unearthed: The Aboriginal Tasmanians of Kangaroo Island*, by Rebe Taylor (Wakefield Press, Revised edition 2008). The first officially documented visit to Kangaroo Island was by Captain Matthew Flinders, who anchored there in 1802. He was followed by Captain Baudin of France less than a year later. Each spent some time exploring the island.

Flinders found no evidence of human habitation, which probably explains why his crew could walk right up to kangaroos and shoot them in the head for food. Baudin left a pair of pigs and a pair of fowl, whose descendants served as food for many of the sealers, whalers, and others who came to live there from that time onward. Nevertheless, native animals were still hunted and it took only 25 years for the indigenous emu to be extinguished. Taylor characterises the settlers of the precolonial era thus: "The men living in skins on Kangaroo Island—perhaps there were about thirty of them in the 1820s—were mostly English. Some were Irish or Scottish, and a small minority came from other places; all but a few were white. They arrived mostly in their twenties—a pack of young men full of bravado who had already seen the hard side of life." (pp30-31) A contemporary newspaper reported that they lived in brush huts and houses made from logs and bark: 'Thirty men and forty black women, independent of a numerous progeny, contrive to make themselves quite comfortable in their snug retreat.' (Australian, March 1826).

The aboriginal cosmology, death and gathering of babies-to-be around the yacca

Archaeologists now believe aboriginal people inhabited Kangaroo Island about 5,000 years ago, before rising sea levels cut it off from the rest of the Australian continent. After that event, the island remained significant in the belief system of nearby mainland tribes. The myths outlined in my novel are among many documented by Philip A. Clarke in *The Aboriginal Australian Cosmic Landscape* (2014), published in the Journal of Astronomical History and Heritage. Vol.17, no.3, pp.307–335.

Horseshoe buying by Germans

There were in fact German agents who travelled through Australia offering to buy old horseshoes.

Germans in South Australia

For further reading about the strong influence of the German-Australian community on South Australian history, I recommend *Germans*, Peter Monteath (Editor), Wakefield Press 2011. This book provides excellent chapters on individuals, events and issues.

Hans Heysen
The well-known artist Heysen lived in the Adelaide Hills. His paintings made a significant impact on the general culture of Australia, most particularly in his own state. For a good short biography and further references, see *The Australian Dictionary of Biography*, online at:
http://adb.anu.edu.au/biography/heysen-sir-wilhelm-ernst-hans-6657

Verran & Homburg
The South Australian Commissioner of Public Works (Hon. R. Butler) and the Attorney General (Hon. H. Homburg) did in fact make a tour of Kangaroo Island in January 1913. *The Register*, 11th September 1913 edition, contains a detailed report of their experience and observations. Homburg himself, like his father before him, was a prominent example of the accomplishments of many in the German-Australian community of the State. He was to suffer for his ancestry during the First World War, when his office was raided by soldiers with fixed bayonets. He subsequently resigned from his position. More about him and his family can be read in *The Australian Dictionary of Biography*, online at
http://adb.anu.edu.au/biography/homburg-hermann-robert-7069

The Yacca species, harvesting methods, and products
The Kangaroo Island yacca is one of the twenty-eight known Xanthorrhoea species. In many parts of Australia, the common name is 'grasstree', but South Australians tend to retain the name 'yacca'. The plants grow very slowly, up to 25 mm per year, and the lifespan may reach six centuries. The Kangaroo Island variety can reach four metres in height. The plant was a valuable resource for the aborigines. The tall flower-stalks were used to make spears; various parts were excellent food; other parts could be used for fire drills and tinder. Today the yacca is protected by law on Kangaroo Island; only a small amount of gum extraction by licensed companies is permitted. Here is a link to more detailed information about the Xanthorrhoea plants:
https://www.anbg.gov.au/gardens/education/progr
ams/Aboriginal-plantuse.pdf

The yacca gum trade
The laborious method of harvesting the gum from between the bases of the leaves in the summer heat is said to be the origin of the Australian vernacular term 'hard yakka', meaning tough work. The process described in the novel for extracting the gum destroyed the whole plant, but some years later a new technique was devised which left it growing. The yacca gum trade was banned by the Australian government soon after the start of the First World War, to prevent material aid reaching enemy hands.

The Kangaroo Island dunnart
This little creature, which uses the lowest leaves of the yacca as a shelter, has managed to survive the damage to its habitat, which occurred in the earlier years of the twentieth century. The protection of the yacca has left the island with small but significant numbers of dunnarts.

The push for preservation on Kangaroo Island
While there was a certain amount of protection of the western end of Kangaroo Island in the early twentieth century, the political support later grew and brought about the far more extensive and rigorous conservation measures in force today.

Motor transport
The Maxwell Tourer was chosen randomly for the car used by Verran and Homburg in this story. The South Australian government was certainly beginning to use motor transport at that time, but I could not ascertain which makes or models it actually bought. The term 'lorry' was used generally in South Australia at the time of the story, and 'truck' was applied to the railway units. Sometime after the First World War, the latter term gradually came to refer to both.

*

If you enjoyed this engaging story by Stephen Crabbe, read his first novel, *Song of Australia*, also available in paperback wherever good books are sold online.

Stephen Crabbe